EVA'S JOURNEY

'[Judi Curtin is] an author with a huge following ... *Eva's Journey* is a story told with her trademark wit and warmth' *Sunday Independent*

'Another cracker about friends and family from Limerick's writing legend.' *Irish Independent*

'A charming, topical story about what really matters in life.' *Bookfest*

'Fabulous book, everyone should read it.' *Bookster Reviews*

JUDI CURTIN grew up in Cork and now lives in Limerick where she is married with three children. Judi is the author of the best-selling 'Alice & Megan' series; with Roisin Meaney, she is also the author of *See If I Care*, and she has written three novels, *Sorry, Walter, From Claire to Here* and *Almost Perfect*. Her books have been translated into Serbian, Portuguese and German.

The 'Alice & Megan' series

Alice Next Door

Alice Again

Don't Ask Alice

Alice in the Middle

Bonjour Alice

Alice & Megan Forever

Alice to the Rescue

Alice & Megan's Cookbook

Other books

See If I Care (with Roisin Meaney)

Praise for the 'Alice & Megan' series

'If you like Jacqueline Wilson, then you'll love Judi Curtin!'
Primary Times

'Rising star Judi Curtin's "Alice" books celebrate friendship, humour and loyalty.' *Sunday Independent*

Judi Curtin

THE O'BRIEN PRESS
DUBLIN

First published 2010 by The O'Brien Press Ltd,
12 Terenure Road East, Rathgar, Dublin 6, Ireland.
Tel: +353 1 4923333; Fax: +353 1 4922777
E-mail: books@obrien.ie
Website: www.obrien.ie
Reprinted 2010, 2011.

ISBN: 978-1-84717-224-2

A catalogue record for this title is available from the British Library

3 4 5 6 7 8
11 12 13 14

The O'Brien Press receives
assistance from

Layout and design: The O'Brien Press Ltd
Cover illustration: Woody Fox
Printed and bound in by UK by CPI Cox and Wyman Ltd.
The paper used in this book is produced using pulp from managed forests.

For Dan, Brian, Ellen and Annie.

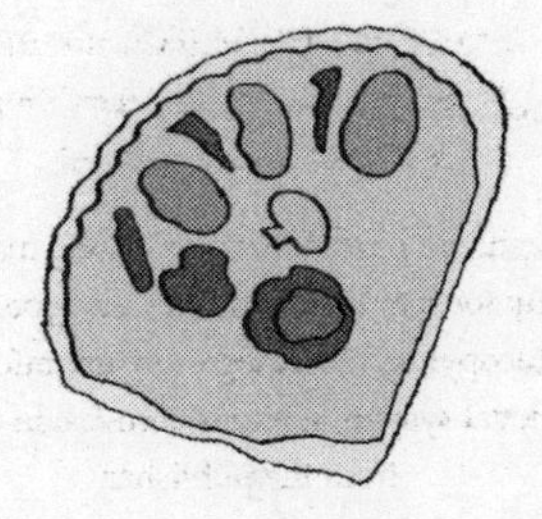

Chapter One

'What about bowling?' suggested Mum. 'Or you could go to the cinema.'

I laughed so much that my mascara started to run.

'That's sooo last year,' I scoffed. 'Bowling and cinema parties are for losers. I want a pamper party. Pamper parties are where it's at these days.'

'I'm not really sure ......' began Mum.

I didn't care that Mum wasn't sure. I was sure, and that was all that mattered.

So, when my twelfth birthday came around, I treated fifteen of my best friends to a superluxurious pamper day in a fancy hotel near my house.

It was totally, totally fantastic.

First of all we had a swim. When we were tired of swimming, we lay on loungers by the side of the pool reading glossy magazines and talking about stuff.

After that, it was time to get our hair and faces done. When my hair was blow-dried, all the other girls said that it made my new highlights look really cool.

My favourite part of the day was when we got our nails painted. Everyone else had to settle for a boring old French manicure, but because I was the birthday girl, I got super-cool gel nails, with a perfect tiny crystal set into each one.

After that, my mum picked us up, and we went to my all-time favourite restaurant for a pizza. I couldn't eat very well because, trust me, it is not easy to hold a pizza without damaging your new gel nails. I didn't care though. It's important to get your priorities right.

When there was nothing left except crusts of pizza and half-glasses of flat lemonade cocktails, the lights went dim and one of the waiters carried out the biggest birthday cake I have ever seen. It said *Happy Birthday, Eva* in huge silver letters and there were sparklers all around the edge. Everyone said stuff like 'Ooooh,' and 'Aaaaah,' and 'Wow.'

By this time I was smiling so much, I thought my face was going to crack open. I *so* love being the centre of attention!

My friends had only sung the first line of 'Happy Birthday' when the sparklers set off the fire alarms, and we all had to run outside screaming.

I didn't mind.

It made sure that no one would forget my party – ever.

☆ ♥ ♡

That night, Victoria, my very best friend in the whole world, came to sleep over at my place. We spent ages on the new computer I'd got for my birthday, and after that we lay on my window-seat and listened to my new MP3 player.

Victoria likes the exact same kind of music as I do. Actually, we like *all* the same things. That's how we met. We started pony club on the same day, years and years ago, when we were both around five years old. All the other girls wanted to ride the chestnut ponies, but I spotted a sleek, black mare looking out of her stall at the other side of the yard. I ran over and stretched up to stroke her nose.

'You're the most beautiful,' I whispered. 'I'm going to go on you.'

Just then I noticed another girl standing there.

'I'm Victoria,' she said, smiling at me, 'and this is Velvet. The instructor said I can ride her.'

I thought of stamping my foot and crying to get my own way, but before I could work myself up to it, Victoria just smiled and said, 'We can take turns if you want,' and that's what we did.

Even though Victoria goes to school in the middle of town, and I go to a private school five miles away, it doesn't matter. We're very, very best friends.

☆ ♥ ♡

Much later, Victoria sighed as she settled in to the spare bed in my bedroom.

'I think that's the best party I've ever, ever been to,' she said.

I didn't argue. How could I, when I knew she was right?

'But I've been looking forward to your party for so long,' she moaned. 'What have I got to look forward to now?'

I didn't have to think before answering.

'What about our pony club trip?' I said.

'That's going to be so much fun.'

'Oh, yeah. I wonder where we're going this year. I hope it's France. I'd totally love to go there.'

'No. France is sooo boring. I'd prefer Germany, or maybe Spain.'

'Whatever. I just wish they'd hurry up and announce it, so we can start looking forward to it properly.'

I snuggled deeper under my duvet.

'Mmm … me too,' I said. 'Now I'm going to sleep. All that beautifying is tiring work.'

'Know what, Eva Gordon?' said Victoria.

'What?' I asked, trying not to yawn.

'It doesn't seem fair. Your life is so perfect. It's like you're living in a fairy-tale. How come bad things never happen to you?'

I giggled.

'Something bad happened last week. Remember when I was going to that party, and before I got my hair straighteners warmed up, there was a power cut? And I had to go to the party with wavy hair? That was bad, wasn't it?'

Victoria giggled too.

'Apart from that total disaster, do you think you might be the luckiest girl in the whole world?'

'Yes. I think I might be.'

'Oh, and one more thing,' she said.

'What?' I said, failing to hold back the yawn this time.

'If you weren't so nice, I'd totally hate you.'

I smiled into the darkness.

'Lucky I'm nice, so,' I said, not really sure if it was true.

✫ ♥ ♡

Victoria was already asleep, and I was just drifting into my first dream of the night, when my bedroom door opened. A figure came over and sat on the edge of my bed.

'Happy birthday, Princess.'

I sat up and hugged my dad, but then I pulled quickly away. I'd forgotten that I was supposed to be cross with him.

'You missed my whole birthday,' I said, in the coldest voice I could manage.

'I'm sorry, Eva,' he said. 'It wasn't my fault. My meeting ran late, and then I missed my connecting flight in London. I got here as soon as I could. You know how busy I am at work, don't you?'

I didn't answer. Years and years ago, before I was even born, Dad used to be a carpenter, but now he ran his own building company. He earned heaps of money, but it meant he was away a lot.

'You forgive me, don't you?' asked Dad.

I wasn't letting him off that easily.

'You missed my birthday last year too.'

He sighed.

'I know. I was in Berlin, wasn't I?'

I shook my head.

'No, that was two years ago. Last year you were entertaining clients in Dublin, and you couldn't get away.'

He hugged me again.

'I'm really sorry. Anyway, I brought you a little something to make up for it.'

I flicked on my light excitedly. I'd already got heaps of presents, but that didn't matter.

What girl can have enough stuff?

Dad fished around in all of his suit pockets, teasing me, before he pulled out a tiny blue box.

'Omigod,' I whispered.

I didn't need to open it – I already recognised the packaging.

I held the present in my hand for a few seconds, enjoying the feeling of not knowing exactly what was inside. Then I ripped off the ribbon, and opened the box. Inside was a tiny silver chain, and on the chain there were two hearts – one silver, and one slightly smaller pinky-gold one.

'Oh, Dad,' I sighed. 'I think that's the most beautiful necklace I have ever, ever seen.'

Dad smiled.

'So I'm forgiven?'

I nodded.

'Of course you are.'

Dad stood up and walked towards the door. Then he stopped.

'You know, Princess, I am very, very sorry I wasn't here for your big day. Next year it will be different. I promise.'

Then he turned and went out, closing the door softly behind him.

Next year it will be different.

Boy, how those words turned out to be true!

Chapter Two

Over the next month or two, the changes happened so slowly, that at first I didn't really notice them.

Dad had always worked very long hours. Now he left home even earlier than before, and got back even later.

When he was at home though, he still hugged me and called me his princess.

He still read too many newspapers.

He still told totally unfunny jokes.

And so I thought everything was just fine.

And then one day, Dad came in from work, and it was like a dark cloud had come over the sun. For the first time in ages, I looked at him closely. He noticed that I was staring at him, and he smiled, but it didn't work. His eyes were blank, like there was something missing – or like there was something else there, something so big that he couldn't see me properly any more.

After that, I noticed that Mum and Dad were fighting a lot. Of course they tried not to argue in front of me, but even in a big house like ours, there's only so much you can hide.

Other times, when I'd come in to a room, I'd find Mum and Dad clinging to each other like they were lost in the middle of the ocean, and that without each other they'd slowly sink to the bottom. That was so gross and scary that I began to wish they'd start fighting again.

Often when I got home from school, Mum's eyes were red. When she saw me, she'd smile a big watery smile.

'Peeling onions again,' she'd say, rubbing her red eyes with the back of her hand.

What could I say to that?

Even if we had onion soup for breakfast, lunch and dinner, Mum wouldn't need that many onions, but I *so* wasn't arguing.

After all, if I told her I didn't believe her, I'd have to ask her what was really wrong. And what is the point of asking questions when you absolutely don't want to hear the answer?

☆ ♥ ♡

One day, when Victoria and I got to pony club, there was a new black pony there. We both ran over and began to stroke her smooth, shiny neck.

'Omigod,' I said. 'She's almost as beautiful as Velvet.'

(Poor Velvet was too old to ride now, and she spent her time resting in a field behind the stables.)

Just then the instructor came over.

'Isn't she a beauty?' she said. 'Her name's Jewel. Which one of you wants to ride her today?'

Victoria and I looked at each other and grinned.

'We're going to take turns,' we said together.

'You two,' said the instructor laughing, and she helped us to saddle up for our morning's riding.

Later, Victoria and I went outside to wait for our mums to pick us up. While we'd been riding, I'd managed to forget about the troubles at home, but now they all came flooding back.

'Can I tell you something,' I said.

Victoria turned to me.

'Course you can,' she said. 'What is it?'

I took a deep breath, but found that I didn't know how to begin.

Dad looks worried?

Mum cries a lot?

It all sounded too vague and too stupid. And besides, I was supposed to be the one with the ideal life, so how could I admit that things might not be quite so perfect after all?

'Well?' said Victoria after a minute.

I tried to smile.

'I still miss Velvet,' I said.

'Me too,' said Victoria. 'Let's come early next week, so that we can go and visit her.'

Just then I saw Mum's jeep coming along the road, and that was the end of that conversation.

✯ ❤ ♔

The first big change hit my life like a party-popper exploding in my face. It happened over dinner one evening. For a change, Dad was there, but no one was saying much. It was like there was a cold, grey fog hanging over the table.

'So, Mum,' I said, when I couldn't take the silence any more. 'When are you going to book the flights to New York for our shopping trip? And don't forget we need to book two suitcases each this time. I've promised all my friends that I'll bring them back something.'

Mum looked at Dad, before turning to me with the bright, false smile that seemed to be her new favourite expression.

'I think we'll give New York a miss this year, Eva. What do you think?'

I gasped.

'I think that's a totally pathetic idea. We *have* to go on our shopping trip. If we don't, what am I supposed to wear for the next six months?'

'How about some of the clothes in your three very large wardrobes?'

'But all those clothes are totally ancient. You can't expect me to......' I gave a sudden laugh. 'Hey, you nearly got me there. That was quite funny actually.'

Mum wasn't laughing. She was still wearing that stupid smile that looked like she'd painted it on.

'You're kidding, right?' I said uncertainly.

Mum shook her head.

'Wrong.'

'But ...'

There were so many 'buts', I didn't know where to begin.

Mum folded her arms.

'Listen Eva,' she began. 'There's something you need to know. You see— '

'No,' said Dad so suddenly that Mum and I both jumped. 'Not now. Now's not the time to tell her.'

'So when is the time?'

Dad sighed.

'I don't know. But she's just a little girl. There's no need to burden her with our worries. Let her alone for a while.'

'Hello?' I said. 'Remember me? My name is Eva. I'm your daughter. And I'm not a little girl – I'm twelve years old. And also, in case you haven't noticed. I'm still in the room.'

Now both of them turned to stare at me.

'There are just a few things going on in Dad's business at the moment,' said Mum. 'So it's not a good time for planning a New York shopping trip.'

Now Dad put on a fake smile to match the one that was once again plastered all over Mum's face.

'You don't have to worry, Princess,' he said. 'It'll all sort itself out in time.'

Did I believe him?

Not for one single second.

✯ ❤ ♡

The next big change happened a week or two after that.

Mum and I were in the kitchen. Mum was at the cooker, stirring the dinner, and I was sitting at the island trying to look like I was studying for a history test.

Then the door opened and Dad walked in.

'Hi, darling,' Mum said without looking up. 'I didn't hear your car in the drive.'

‘That’s because my car isn’t in the drive,’ said Dad.

They weren’t such bad words. Dad’s car could have been in the garage, or he could have lent it to one of his friends. But something in the way Dad said those words made me drop my history book. It fell to the floor in a loud rustle of flapping pages, like it was an injured bird trying to fly.

For one second I wished that I was a bird.

I wished I could fly far away from this scene that was unfolding in front of me.

Dad had gone to sit at the kitchen table. He was pale and old-looking.

When had he started to look old?

And why hadn’t I noticed it before?

Mum and I both walked towards him.

Dad put his head in his hands, like he couldn’t bring himself to look at us.

‘It’s gone,’ he said, through his closed fingers.

'The car is gone. They came today and took it away.'

Why wasn't he angry?

Still, I could be plenty angry enough for the two of us.

'Who came?' I asked. 'Who took it away? How can someone come and just take your car away? Have you called the police? Do you want me to pass you the phone?'

Dad looked up, but I wished he hadn't. The look in his eyes scared me more than anything I'd ever seen before.

'You don't understand, Princess,' he said. 'I borrowed money to buy the car, and now I can't make the repayments. So the bank can take possession of the car. It's the law. There's nothing I can do about it.'

I felt like crying.

Dad loved his car.

I loved his car.

I loved the sleek, silver body-work.

I loved the smell and the feel of the leather seats.

I loved the way people stared at us whenever we drove it down the street.

But I *so* didn't love the look in my dad's eyes, and I knew I had to be strong.

'It's just a car, Dad,' I said. 'It's no big deal. And Mum still has the jeep if we want to go anywhere. And luckily your office isn't far from here. It'll probably be good for you to walk there every day. And.....'

I rambled on for a while, and then I stopped.

Suddenly I realised that I was missing the point. This wasn't just about the car.

I took a deep breath and asked another question, the one I should have been smart enough to ask in the first place.

'Why can't you make the repayments?'

'Because I haven't got enough money.'

His voice was hoarse and scary.

'But you've got heaps of money. You're rich. You're richer than any of my friends' dads. You're ...'

I stopped talking. I didn't feel sure of anything any more. Dad put his face in his hands again, and Mum just stood there, still holding the wooden spoon, which was dripping curry sauce all over the shiny white floor tiles.

She put her other hand on Dad's back, and rubbed it gently, like he was a baby who'd drunk its bottle too fast.

'I'm sorry, Eva,' she said. 'We didn't know how to tell you. Dad's business has been doing very badly lately. It's not his fault. The recession has taken everyone by surprise. Things are going to have to change around here. We can't afford to live the way we used to.'

'No!' I shouted the single word.

I wasn't stupid. I listened to the television and

the radio. Sometimes I even read the headlines on the newspapers. I'd heard all about the recession. I'd heard about girls whose parents had lost their jobs. I *knew* times were hard.

But that was all about other people. That kind of thing wasn't about us.

We were rich.

We were happy.

We were invincible.

'No!' I said again, not quite as loudly as before.

Mum hugged Dad, and then she came over and hugged me.

'I'm sorry, Eva,' she said. 'You can say "no" all you like, but I'm afraid it won't change a single thing.'

I pulled away from her. I went to the front door, and looked out to the space where Dad's car was supposed to be.

Was I hoping that I could magic it back by just wishing?

'No!' I said again to the cold dark air.

This wasn't going to happen.

I simply wasn't going to allow it.

Chapter Three

Victoria called over later. I rushed her through the kitchen so quickly that she didn't have time to notice Mum and Dad sitting at the table looking like their world was collapsing around their ears.

Victoria followed me up to my room. I played with the controls of my MP3 player, and managed to pretend that everything was OK for about thirty seconds.

'What's wrong, Eva?' asked Victoria.

'How do you mean?' I asked, still half-hoping that I could bluff her.

'You're too quiet,' she said. 'It's making me nervous.'

I jumped up, pulled a few books from my shelves, and threw them on to the floor where they landed with a huge clatter.

'Better?' I said. 'Now I'm not quiet any more.'

Now she looked even more nervous.

'Don't act crazy,' she said. 'I'm serious, Eva. What's wrong?'

I hesitated.

I wasn't used to telling people my problems.

Well actually, that's not really true. The truth is, I wasn't used to having problems to tell people about.

But I badly needed to tell someone, so I took a deep breath and told Victoria everything.

'Wow,' she said in the end.

'That's it? Wow?'

She looked embarrassed. 'What do you want me to say?'

Even though it wasn't one bit funny, I giggled.

'I don't know. Maybe you should say that

everything's going to be OK or something.'

Victoria put on a serious expression.

'Know what, Eva?' she said. 'I think everything's going to be OK.'

'But how is it going to be OK?'

She hesitated.

'How am I supposed to know?'

I made a face and she tried again.

'Oh, I know,' she said after a while. 'Your Dad's business will start to improve. He'll have enough money to buy back his car, or maybe he'll have enough to buy an even better one, and then you can all live happily ever after.'

'You really think so?'

Suddenly Victoria gave a huge grin.

'I don't just *think* things will get better – I *know* it. Because I've just had a great idea. You don't have to sit here fretting,' she said. 'You can help your dad.'

'How?'

'You could try to manage without pocket money for a few weeks. And you could get a job too, and then you could save up money to help to pay off your dad's debts.'

'What kind of job?'

'You could do baby-sitting. You like children and they like you.'

'And I could get a paper round after school too,' I said.

'And you could walk dogs for people who are too busy to do it themselves.'

'And I could muck out the stables after pony club.'

Suddenly it all seemed possible.

Victoria grabbed a paper and pen from my desk. She made four columns, and wrote lots of figures.

'See,' she said in the end, holding the page towards me. 'If you work really hard, look how much you could earn every week!'

I looked at the page, and knew that it was hopeless. I'd heard Mum and Dad mention numbers that made Victoria's calculations look pathetic. I crumpled up the page and dropped it onto my bed.

'It's no use,' I said. 'Even if I walked every dog in the country, and minded every child, and delivered papers twenty-four seven, it wouldn't make any difference. Dad owes too much money.'

Victoria picked up the page, and threw it into the bin.

'Sorry,' she said. 'But maybe there's some other way you could help?'

I shook my head.

'Thanks, Victoria, but this is too big for us. There's nothing we can do.'

She came over and hugged me, but I pulled away.

'You can go if you want. I don't mind if you

don't want to be my friend,' I said.

Victoria picked up a pillow and whacked me with it. At other times, it would quickly have turned into a full-scale pillow fight, but not now. I turned away, trying not to cry.

Victoria put the pillow down.

'You idiot,' she said. 'I'm not your friend because you're rich. I'm your friend … well I'm your friend for all kinds of reasons. You're the most generous person I know. You're always giving me stuff. And remember the time, years ago, when you gave that little girl up the road your two favourite Barbies because she didn't have any of her own?'

'I'd forgotten about that,' I said.

'I bet she hasn't,' said Victoria quickly. 'I bet she still loves you like the sister she never had.'

'She's got three sisters,' I said, and we both laughed for a second.

Then Victoria continued.

'I'm your friend because I like doing stuff with you. I'm your friend because you're fun to be around.'

I should probably have interrupted her, but how could I?

Who doesn't like hearing good stuff about themselves?

'You don't have to worry, Eva,' she said. 'I'll always like you. I'll still like you even if you end up being the poorest person in the whole country.'

I looked up at her. Her big, blue eyes were wide open, and I knew for sure she was telling the truth.

'Thanks, Victoria,' I said. 'It's really nice of you to say all that stuff.'

There was still a problem though. If I was poor, Victoria might still like me – but would I still like myself?

I'd been rich all my life.

It was all I knew.

I was used to being the girl who had everything.

How could I live if I turned into the girl who had hardly anything at all?

Chapter Four

For a while, it looked like maybe things weren't going to change that much.

Mum and Dad seemed a bit more relaxed now that they had told me the truth. They were really nice to each other, and to me. Sometimes they smiled, and once or twice they even laughed.

I got used to not seeing Dad's car in the driveway.

Dad even got used to walking to work.

In the mornings, he set off wearing running shoes with his suit, and it made him look a tiny bit cool – almost like one of those grungy rock stars.

Then one Saturday morning, I went downstairs, to find Mum and Dad sitting at the kitchen table, looking more serious than ever.

'Sit down, Eva,' said Mum.

'We need to talk to you,' said Dad.

It didn't take a genius to figure out that this wasn't going to be about what kind of cereal I wanted for breakfast.

I sat down and waited.

And waited.

Mum looked at Dad and Dad looked at Mum and then they both looked at the floor.

It reminded me of the time we were on holidays in Mexico and there was an ice-cold swimming pool in the garden of our villa. I used to stand on the edge of that pool for ages, trying to get the courage to jump in. I knew that it was going to hurt like crazy, and yet I wanted to get it over with.

I sooo wanted to get this talk over with.

'Eva, Dad and I have decided ......' began Mum.

'...... that we have to sell the house,' said Dad in the end.

I could feel my whole body relaxing.

Was that all?

'The house in Tuscany? You told me that months ago. Remember you told me it was getting too hard to find someone to look after it when we weren't there?'

Even as I said the words, I knew that Mum and Dad hadn't told me the truth about our Italian home.

Was that the first sign of trouble, and I hadn't been smart enough to see it?

'Sorry, Eva,' said Dad, reading my mind. 'We didn't want to worry you by telling you what the real problem was.'

'The house in Tuscany was sold a long time ago,' said Mum. 'We just couldn't afford to keep it any more.'

Suddenly I remembered something else that had gone right over my head a few weeks earlier.

'Teresita didn't stop cleaning our house because she had to go back to the Philippines to look after her sick sister, did she?'

Mum shook her head slowly.

'Sorry, Eva. We couldn't afford to pay Teresita any more, so she got a job at the other side of town. I don't even know if Teresita has a sister.'

I felt like an idiot.

'I made Teresita's imaginary sister a Get-Well card,' I said. 'How totally embarrassing is that?'

Mum sighed.

'I know, darling. And Dad and I felt bad about that. It's just that we didn't know how to tell you the truth.'

I felt like giving Mum and Dad a hard time about telling so many lies, but one look at their downcast faces told me that would have been unfair.

Then I thought of something much, much worse.

'If the house in Tuscany was sold ages ago, then what house were you talking about selling just now?' I gasped with the horror of it, and then tried to continue. 'You're not ......? You wouldn't ......? You can't mean ......?'

Mum nodded sadly.

'I'm afraid we're going to have to sell *this* house. We're selling Castleville.'

'But you can't sell Castleville,' I protested. 'It's our house. It's where we live. It's our home. I've never lived anywhere else. I don't want to live anywhere else.'

Dad rubbed my arm.

'Don't you think we know all that?' he said. 'This isn't easy for any of us.'

'So don't do it then,' I said.

Dad sighed.

'We don't have a choice. The business is in

ruins. We can't afford to live here anymore.'

Suddenly I had a great idea.

'But there's a recession on,' I said. 'This is one of the biggest houses in town. If we can't afford to live here, then who else can?'

Mum gave a small smile. 'There's always someone. Dad and I have been to the estate agents already. They think they have a buyer. We won't get anything like the full value of the house, but we're not in a position to argue. We just have to sell. And when everything is finalised, we can rent a smaller house, not too far from here, so you can still be near Victoria.'

Suddenly I had another idea.

'Dad's business might be in trouble, but there's still your job, Mum. Why can't we live here on what you earn?'

Mum sighed.

'You know my job is only part-time. It hardly pays for the food we eat.'

I grinned.

'I can help with that,' I said. 'I'll eat extra at school. I'll have second servings of everything – third servings even, if they'll let me. I'll eat so much at school, that you won't have to pay for any food for me at home. I'll even skip breakfast. I'll ......'

I stopped talking. Mum was looking at Dad in a way that was making me very nervous.

I gulped. My school had one of the best canteens in the whole country. A celebrity chef visited one time, and we all got his autograph. There was a programme on TV saying that our school served better food than most restaurants.

'Oh, Mum, Dad,' I wailed. 'Please don't tell me that we can't afford to pay for school dinners any more.'

Dad went pale. He looked at Mum who nodded so slightly that I almost missed it. Then he took a deep breath.

'It's not just the dinners, Eva,' he said. 'I'm afraid we can't afford the fees for The Abbey any more either. You're going to have to leave your school.'

I shook my head, wanting to make all the bad stuff go away. This couldn't be happening. I won't pretend that school was my favourite place in the whole world, but I knew that The Abbey was the best one around. (That's why I spent forty-five minutes on a bus to get there every morning.)

Mum came over and hugged me.

'We're sorry, darling, but it's all arranged. We've already spoken to the principal. You'll be leaving at the end of this term.'

I thought quickly. 'But that's only two weeks away.'

Dad nodded. 'But look on the bright side. Even though it's the middle of a school year, we've managed to get you in to a new school.'

Ha. Look on the bright side – easy for him to say.

Then I realised there *was* a bright side.

'Hey,' I said. 'I can go to Victoria's school. It'll be kind of cool being at school with my best friend at last. And she says her school's not too bad really. She says …'

I stopped talking. Why were Mum and Dad looking at me like that?

Why were there tears in Mum's eyes, even though there wasn't a single onion in sight?

'We thought of sending you to Victoria's school,' said Dad. 'It's a good school, and they don't charge fees. That would have been just perfect.'

Would have been perfect?

'But there's no room there,' continued Mum.

'But there are only three schools within reach of here,' I said. 'If we can't afford The Abbey any more, and Victoria's school is full, that only leaves ……'

Dad stood up and came over to me. His hand

on my shoulder was warm and strong. It was the hand of a man who should be able to put things right.

But he wasn't putting things right.

He nodded slowly.

'That only leaves Woodpark School. It's all sorted. You start there straight after the holidays.'

'No way,' I said. 'That's just not going to happen. Woodpark school is ... well ... it's not the kind of school that girls like me go to.'

Dad pulled his hand away from my shoulder.

'Eva,' he said angrily. 'It's time for you to stop being so precious. If Woodpark isn't the kind of school that girls like you go to, maybe you'd better think about becoming the kind of girl that goes to Woodpark school.'

I gulped.

I liked the kind of girl I was already.

I *so* didn't want to change.

But Dad was looking at me in a way that made

me decide that, for once, arguing with him wasn't going to be a good idea.

I knew for sure that this wasn't going to be the kind of argument that I was used to having with my dad – the kind that ended up with Dad apologising and buying me an expensive present.

So I smiled my brightest smile.

'That's cool,' I said. 'My life was a bit boring anyway. Change is good. Change is exciting.'

I ignored Mum and Dad's puzzled looks. I kissed them both on the cheek, and I skipped out of the room like I'd just heard the best news ever.

Then I went up to my room, threw myself on to my bed and cried until my pure silk sheets were soaked through.

✯ ♥ ♡

As soon as I stopped crying, I phoned Victoria.

'We've got to move house, and I have to change schools,' I said, before she even had time to say 'hello'.

'Oh,' she said.

There was a long silence before she recovered.

'A new house will be fun,' she said brightly. 'Remember before when you said it was boring living in the same house all your life?'

'Yeah,' I conceded. 'But I didn't mean it – not really.'

'And a new school – that'll be exciting.'

I tried not to cry at the injustice of it all.

'A new fancy boarding school would be exciting,' I said. 'But we're not talking about a fancy boarding school. I've got to go to . . . Woodpark.'

This time the silence was even longer. I was beginning to wonder if Victoria had fainted at the news, when she spoke again.

'Woodpark's meant to be . . . . . . OK,' she said slowly.

'No, it's *not*,' I said angrily. 'I've heard some of the girls in my school talk about it. They say it's really rough and scary.'

'What do they know?' said Victoria. 'They probably just made that stuff up. Anyway, my mum went to Woodpark, and she turned out OK.'

'That was hundreds of years ago,' I said. 'And it so doesn't count.'

Victoria decided it was time to change the subject.

'Do you want to hang out for a while? You can come over here if you like.'

'No,' I said. 'Why don't you come here?'

I didn't finish the sentence –

– *while you still can?*

☆ ♥ ♡

A few days later, Mum sold her jeep and came home in a tiny, battered old car.

'I really like this car,' she said brightly, as she patted the fading red paint. 'It's got personality.'

I didn't answer. I didn't look for personality in a car – all I wanted was satnav and a super sound system and leather seats.

That wasn't so much to ask for, was it?

A week after that, Dad's business closed down completely.

When he came home and told me, I wasn't even surprised.

Nothing could surprise me any more.

I hugged him. 'Don't worry,' I said. 'I'm sure you'll find another job soon.'

He nodded. 'I'm sure I will,' he said.

I wondered why we were bothering to tell lies, since we were both so bad at it.

✫ ♥ ♡

Our house was sold very quickly. That's the way the new owners wanted it, and Mum and Dad didn't argue. I knew how they felt. How can you enjoy something when you're just sitting there, waiting for it to be taken away from you forever?

✫ ♥ ♡

I'm not going to say much about the day we moved out – not because I don't want to, but because it's all a bit of a blur.

I can remember lots of packing cases and lots of tears.

I can remember Dad telling me to grow up, which so wasn't fair, as he's always saying that I'm still his baby girl.

I can remember the slam of the front door, as we left for the last time.

I can remember Mum, Dad and me piling into Mum's small red car.

I can remember the crunch of the car tyres on the gravel.

I can remember turning back for a last look at the name-plaque on the gate post – Castleville House.

I can remember the dull clang of the electric gates as they closed behind us for the very last time.

I can remember the short, silent car journey.

I can remember pulling up outside the small,

ugly house we had rented.

I can remember thinking that my life was over.

Chapter Five

Soon it was my last day in The Abbey. My form teacher, Mrs Reynolds, was really nice. She shook my hand as I walked out after my last class.

'You're a bright girl, Eva,' she said. 'You'll do well wherever you go.'

'But I don't want to go anywhere' I felt like crying. *'I just want to stay here.'*

But that would have been too weird, so I just gave Mrs Reynolds' hand one last shake, and went outside to catch my bus.

Most of my friends were in the school yard. We all hugged and kissed and cried.

They all called after me as I climbed on to the

school bus for the very last time.

'We'll still be friends.'

'Let's keep in touch.'

'We'll never forget you.'

Most of them did remember me – for the first few days anyway. But they all lived too far away to be proper friends. Even though their fathers' cars hadn't been towed away by evil tow-truck men, they didn't seem to be able to travel the few miles to visit me during the holidays.

Some of the girls texted me – for the first few days anyway. But I had no credit on my phone, so I couldn't reply – and soon the texts stopped coming.

I didn't take it personally.

But that didn't stop it hurting.

✯ ❤ ♡

The days in the dump that I was supposed to call my new home seemed to go by very slowly. I wandered around the small rooms feeling cross and miserable.

'Go upstairs and unpack some of your boxes,' said Mum one morning. 'You're driving me crazy with your moaning.'

I thought about arguing, but felt sorry when I saw Mum's tired face. This whole thing couldn't have been much fun for her either. So I gave her a quick hug, and then I went upstairs and looked at the boxes stacked in the narrow hallway outside my bedroom.

I tried, I really did. But how can the contents of three wardrobes, two chests of drawers and seven bookshelves, fit into one very small, very narrow cupboard? It was like trying to fit a rugby team into a Mini Cooper – totally impossible.

Dad came in when he heard me crying. He looked at the cupboard that was already stuffed to bursting point, even though I'd only unpacked the first two boxes.

'You'll get used to it,' he said. 'My two brothers

and I had to share a wardrobe about that size.'

'But that was so different,' I said. 'You only owned one set of clothes each.'

'Didn't do us any harm,' he said. 'We survived.'

'But I don't want to just survive,' I wailed. 'I want to live.'

I started to cry again, and Dad came over and hugged me. He always hates to see me cry. He patted my hair.

'There, there, my little Princess,' he said. 'Please stop crying and I'll buy you a ...'

I stopped sobbing and looked up at him hopefully, but he put his hands over his eyes.

'Just stop crying, please,' he said.

☆ ❤ ♡

Then one morning I woke up and realised that the next day I'd be starting my new school.

I lay in bed, looking around my small bedroom; even though I still hated my new home,

I'd have happily locked myself in there forever, if it meant I could have avoided facing in to Woodpark School all on my own.

I was still in my pyjamas when Victoria called over.

'Come on, Eva,' she said. 'It's the last day of the holidays. We should be out having fun.'

'I'm not sure if I mentioned this before – but my life is over,' I said. 'How can you expect me to have fun? I don't do fun any more.'

Victoria ignored me, and I couldn't really blame her. I'd done nothing but moan ever since I'd moved house.

'Come on,' she repeated. 'Let's go.'

'Go where?' I asked sulkily.

'Town?'

'That sounds like loads of fun,' I said bitterly. 'We can stand outside restaurants and smell the food I can't afford to eat. After that we can look in the shop windows at the clothes I can't afford to buy. It'll be a total blast.'

Once again she ignored me.

'We'll go to the park in town. That doesn't cost anything. It's a nice day, and there's always stuff going on in the park.'

I felt like punching her.

Did I *look* like the kind of girl who liked hanging out doing stuff in a park?

But I didn't say this. I had just remembered that this was my new life.

My new life where everything was different.

I pulled on my clothes, called to Mum and Dad that I was going out, and followed Victoria outside.

She was right, it was a nice day, and even though I wouldn't have admitted it to Victoria, being outside did make me feel a bit better.

'I know a short-cut to town,' she said. 'It's just down this street.'

I looked at her, surprised.

'I'm the one who lives here. So how come you're the one who knows the short-cuts?'

She made a face.

'If you spent less time crying in your bedroom, you might get to know the short-cuts too.'

Once again she was right.

'I'm sorry, Victoria,' I said. 'I've been a right pain these last few weeks.'

She smiled at me.

'That's OK. Everyone gets to feel sorry for themselves for a while, and then the time comes when you have to just get on with your life.'

'And I'm guessing that time has come?'

She nodded.

'Exactly.'

I followed her as she led the way through a maze of small streets. Then as we turned a corner, I stumbled on a sign that was propped up against a garden wall. I rubbed my leg, and then bent to pick up the sign that had gone flying into the street.

Madame Margarita it read, in wobbly gold lettering.

Then underneath that, in even wobblier red letters, it said. *I can tell your fortune. The secrets of the future will be yours. For ten euro you can change your life.*

I put the sign back where it had been, wondering for a second why my fingers were stained with red and gold. Then I stood there and looked at the sign for a long time.

'Let's go,' said Victoria.

I shook my head.

'Hang on a sec,' I said. 'Look at this sign. It says you can change your life. Do you have *any* idea how much I need to change my life?'

Victoria sighed.

'I know you want to change your life, but surely you don't believe in that stuff?'

I shrugged.

'I don't know. I used to believe in all kinds of stuff that turned out not to be true. Maybe it's time I found different stuff to believe in.'

Victoria shook her head.

'Forget it, Eva. It's crazy. No-one with a brain believes in fortune tellers, and last time I checked, you had a brain.'

'Thanks,' I muttered.

'And besides,' she continued. 'Even if this Madam Margarita could tell you your future, how would that help you?'

I thought for a minute.

'I just think it would. If I knew how long it would take for my life to get back to normal, maybe I could cope better.'

'But, what if ... what if Madam Margarita told you that your life isn't going to get back to normal? What if this is as good as it gets?'

'Well, at least then I'd know, wouldn't I? You couldn't possibly understand, Victoria. These last few months have been crazy for me. It's like being in one of those fairground crazy-houses – the ground under my feet is suddenly all wobbly. If I don't find something to hold on to, I'm going to go crashing down in a heap. Nothing seems right any more. I want to know what's going to happen next. I *have* to know what's going to happen next.'

Then I put my head down.

'It doesn't matter anyway. It costs ten euro to see Madam Margarita. I don't have ten euro. I don't have ten cents. I don't have any money at all.'

Victoria smiled.

'I have ten euro. I was going to buy you a present in town – to wish you luck for your first day in your new school. You can have the money instead if you like.'

'Really?'

She nodded.

'Really. I still think this whole fortune-telling thing is total rubbish, but if it's what you want ...'

I hugged her.

'It is *so* what I want. Thank you so, so much Victoria. Will you come in with me?'

She shook her head.

'No way. That future stuff freaks me out. The present is more than enough for me to cope with. Here, take the ten euro before I change my mind. And I'll wait out here, just in case Madam Margarita decides to eat you or something.'

'And if she does, will you come in and rescue me?'

Victoria shook her head.

'No! I'd be too scared. But at least I'll be able to go home and tell your parents what happened to you.'

'You're a true friend,' I said, and we both laughed.

Then I took the ten euro from Victoria, and

watched as she went to sit on a wall at the other side of the road.

'You know you could buy a really nice t-shirt with that ten euro,' she called.

'No, thanks,' I called back, and then I walked slowly up the path to Madam Margarita's house.

Chapter Six

I knocked on the door, and stood back as flakes of blue paint fluttered and floated towards the ground. After a minute, I could hear a very weird squeaking noise. I held my breath as the squeaking became louder. Whatever was making the noise was getting closer. I could feel an icy cold shiver run slowly up and down my spine. I turned to look over to Victoria, who just waved cheerfully.

'This is crazy,' I thought. 'What am I doing here?'

Then, just as I turned to go back to my friend, the door opened.

I found myself looking at a woman. Her face

was thin and pale. She had dark hair, and huge brown eyes. She was wearing an ugly blue tracksuit, and runners that were totally last season. She was sitting in a wheelchair.

'What do you want?' she asked.

'I'm sorry for disturbing you,' I said. 'I was looking for Madam Margarita.'

'That's me,' she said.

'You don't look like a fortune-teller,' I said.

'Well, you don't look like a princess,' she shot back.

When I didn't answer, she pointed at my necklace, which said 'Princess' in sparkly pink letters – one of Dad's little jokes, from way back when he still had a sense of humour.

'Ha, ha,' I said. 'Very funny. Not. Anyway, I think I've changed my mind. I don't want my fortune told.'

'No,' she said. 'Don't go. Please. You're my first customer.'

'You mean I'm your first customer today?'

She hesitated. 'Er …… yes.'

I knew she was lying. That's why the red and gold paint had stained my fingers – her sign hadn't even had a chance to dry.

How did I end up with a fortune teller who was on her first day on the job?

'Come in,' she said, wheeling herself backwards into the narrow hall. The squeaking sound started again. It must be awful to have to use a wheel-chair, but surely oiling the wheels occasionally would make it easier to bear?

'Come in,' she said again, smiling this time.

She looked younger when she smiled.

It seemed rude not to follow her, so with a last glance over at Victoria, I stepped in to the hall.

I looked around. I don't know a whole lot about fortune-tellers' houses, but surely they weren't meant to look like this – small and shabby and sad?

Madam Margarita was watching me.

'What were you expecting?' she asked. 'Buckingham Palace?'

I shook my head embarrassed.

'No.' I said quickly. 'It's just that this house is a lot like the one I live in.'

It was the truth.

Madam Margarita didn't comment on this, but her face made it clear that she didn't believe me.

'In there.'

She pointed to a room, and I obediently stepped inside.

'I'll be back in a second,' said Madam Margarita as she closed the door behind me.

I was in a small, untidy room. All of one wall was taken up by a bed. In the middle of the room there was a round table, and one chair.

Before I had made up my mind whether to sit or stand, Madam Margarita was back. Now she was wearing a turban made of cheap-looking shiny fabric, and wrapped around her shoulders was a silver shawl. She looked a bit like a turkey all ready to go into the oven.

'Sit,' she said.

I sat on the only chair, and Madam Margarita wheeled herself so that she was facing me.

She took something from her knees and put it on the table.

'My crystal ball,' she announced.

It looked more like an upside down goldfish bowl. I wondered if there was a poor fish in the kitchen, desperately holding its breath until it could get its home back.

'So you want to know what the future holds for you?'

At first I didn't answer.

This was all too stupid.

If Madam Margarita could tell the future, and could tell how she was going to spend the day, why did she bother getting up out of bed?

If she had such great powers, why didn't she use them to get herself a better life than this one?

But then I figured I was going to have to pay the ten euro now anyway, so I might as well just get on with it.

And besides, behind Madam Margarita's tough expression, there was the hint that maybe she was quite a nice person. Maybe she really could help me.

So I opened my mouth and the words came tumbling out.

'Yes, I want to know my future. You see, things have been really awful lately. My dad's business has closed down, and we have hardly any money, and his car is gone, and Mum's jeep is gone, and we have to drive around in this totally embarrassing old banger, and we had to move house, and I have to go to a new school tomorrow, and I'm really nervous about that, and—'

'Stop!'

Madam Margarita had folded her arms.

'That's all very interesting, Princess, but before you say another word, will you go back outside and read my sign again?'

'You're kidding.'

'No, I'm not. Just do it.'

This was too weird, but for some reason, I found myself doing what she said. I went back outside, leaving the front door open behind me. While I was outside I looked across at Victoria, but she didn't see me. She was busy playing with her phone.

I thought about running across to her.

I thought about forgetting the whole crazy fortune-telling thing.

But instead, I carefully re-read the sign and then I went back inside the shabby house and sat down.

'So,' said Madam Margarita. 'Did you see

where my sign mentions counselling?'

I shook my head. 'No.'

'That's because it's not there. I'm a fortune teller, not a counsellor.'

Then her voice softened, and she sounded almost kind.

'I'm sorry, Princess, but I'm not qualified to be a counsellor. It would be wrong of me to listen to your problems. So why don't you just let me tell your fortune and you can go on your way?'

I nodded, trying to sound braver than I felt.

'Sure,' I said. 'Go right ahead and tell me what the future holds for me. I can take it – I think.'

Chapter Seven

Madam Margarita adjusted her ugly turban, settled herself more comfortably on her chair, and spoke in a whispery voice.

'Cross my palm with silver.'

'What?'

'It means give me the money,' she said in her ordinary voice.

I handed her the ten euro, and she put it into the pocket of her tracksuit.

'Now,' she said. 'Put your hands on the table.'

I did as she said.

She leaned forwards and examined my hands. She looked especially closely at the only nail that still had its gel extension, with the crystal set into it. I don't know why, but I felt like I had to explain myself.

'I got my nails done as a birthday treat.'

Then she looked at my designer hoodie.

'That's one of those fancy jumpers that cost a fortune, isn't it?'

I could feel my face going red.

Was it because my seventy-dollar hoodie was *meant* to be faded and ripped, while clearly Madam Margarita's cheap tracksuit top was faded and ripped from being worn too much?

'Well, sort of,' I replied. 'But I bought this hoodie in America, and they're not so expensive over there.'

She gave a big laugh.

'So you flew all the way to America to save money on a jumper – sounds a bit strange to me.'

I couldn't argue with her – it did sound a bit stupid when she said it like that.

Madam Margarita released my hands, and I quickly sat on them – like I could pretend that they weren't there.

She put her hands around the sides of the crystal ball/goldfish bowl, and gazed into it, like she could actually see something besides the grubby tablecloth underneath.

Her voice went all whispery again.

'I see a lot of things in your future.'

'Like what?'

'Patience, child. Everything's a bit cloudy. It's hard to see clearly.'

No wonder she couldn't see clearly. Her so-called crystal ball was really filthy.

I gazed at the ceiling and waited. A huge cobweb stretched from the doorway right across to the furthest corner of the room.

Suddenly Madam Margarita jumped. She took me by surprise and I jumped too. We both gave nervous laughs.

'I can see lots and lots of things in your future,' she repeated.

This time I knew better than to rush her. In my nervousness, I picked the last remaining crystal from my fingernail. The crystal fell to the floor, and I winced as I saw it slip betweens a crack in the floorboards.

At last, Madam Margarita spoke again.

'I see sadness,' she said. 'I see lots of sadness and disappointment.'

Great, I thought. It didn't take great talent to see that. After all, I'd already told her about my pathetic life.

Then she smiled. I noticed that she had beautiful, even, white teeth. 'And I see happiness. Lots of happiness.'

I waited, but if Madam Margarita could see anything else, it didn't look like she was planning on sharing it with me.

Lots of happiness sounded good, but I needed

to know more.

How long was I supposed to wait before the happiness gig got going?

Was there any way of speeding up the process?

'Er....can you see how exactly I get from the big sadness to the big happiness?' I asked.

Madam Margarita didn't answer at first. She leaned forward with her eyes closed.

Was she thinking about my future?

Or was she falling asleep?

Suddenly her eyes shot open.

'I can see good deeds, and then I can see happiness.'

I grinned. I really liked the sound of that.

'So, what you're saying is, loads of people are going to do good deeds to help me so I can be happy again?'

She shook her head impatiently.

'Are you deliberately misunderstanding me? That's not the way it works. You're the one who has to do the good deeds.'

'Oh,' I said, not liking the sound of that quite so much.

Madam Margarita smiled.

'It's becoming clearer now. I can see you helping people. I can see you helping many people. And then happiness comes to you as gently as the sweet falling rain on a soft spring morning.'

'Sweet falling rain?' I repeated.

Madam Margarita looked at me. 'Too much?'

I nodded. 'Too much.'

'OK,' she said. 'Let's put it into your kind of language. I see you doing loads of good stuff for people, and then you get to be really happy again. How does that sound?'

It sounded fair enough to me, but could it really be that simple?

There were too many possibilities.

'Who am I supposed to do good deeds for?' I

asked. 'How am I supposed to know who to help? Do I have to help old ladies across the road, or do I have to save the rainforests? And how many people do I have to help? If I do one totally amazing good thing, would that be as good as lots of small things?'

Madam Margarita shrugged, and her silver shawl made a loud crinkly noise.

'Nothing is simple. Many people are unhappy. Many people have problems that you could help them with. Wherever there is an opportunity to do something good, just do it. Your reward will come in time.'

I sat there, wondering if she could possibly be right.

In some ways, Madam Margarita seemed like a total fraud.

And yet, there was something in her eyes that made me think she might be telling the truth.

There was a long silence.

A very long, very uncomfortable silence.

'So that's it?' I said in the end.

She nodded.

'That's it. Your session is over.'

I couldn't make up my mind whether I was disappointed or relieved.

Madam Margarita led the way back out into the hall, with her wheels squeaking loudly as she went.

'Hey,' I said suddenly. 'That squeaky noise must drive you crazy. Haven't you got any oil?'

'I think there's some in the shed out the back, but I can't get out there since ... well I can't get out there any more. And everyone else around here is busy all the time.'

I hesitated. It was a lovely sunny day, and I wanted to get back outside to Victoria, but if I was going to spend my life doing good deeds, I figured I might as well get started.

'Tell me exactly where the oil is,' I said.

I went out to the shed and found the oil on the shelf where Madam Margarita had told me it would be. It didn't take long to oil the wheels of her chair, and I got her to wheel herself up and down the hall, making sure I had done it properly.

Madam Margarita smiled.

'That was a little thing to you,' she said. 'But it's a big help to me. Thank you very much.'

Suddenly I felt embarrassed.

'You're welcome,' I said, and I ran outside to my friend.

☆ ♥ ♡

'You were ages,' said Victoria. 'I was starting to get worried.'

I shrugged. 'It didn't seem like long to me.'

'And what did Madam Margarita say? Is your life going to change? Are you going to get rich again?'

'She said ...' I stopped talking.

She said I should do loads of good stuff, and then my life would get better.

How crazy did that sound?

How could I say that to Victoria without sounding like a total idiot?

So I just smiled.

'She didn't say a whole lot,' I said. 'I should have listened to you. I should have kept the money and bought a t-shirt.'

Chapter Eight

Next morning, the door-bell rang while I was having my breakfast. I raced to answer it, wondering if it could possibly be good news.

Was this my reward for oiling the wheels of Madam Margarita's wheelchair?

Was this my fairy godmother, come to rescue me from my rubbish new life?

It was Victoria.

'I've come to wish you luck on your first day in your new school,' she said.

I hugged her.

'That's so, so nice of you,' I said. 'But aren't you going to be late for school now?'

She shook her head.

'It's fine. My dad drove me. He's waiting outside, and he's going to drop me at school on his way to work.'

I felt a sudden stab of jealousy.

Would my dad ever again have a car?

Would he ever again have a job to drive to?

There was a long silence.

'I'm scared,' I said in the end.

'What exactly are you scared of?' she asked.

I shrugged.

'I'm not really sure. The whole thing is just scary. What if the kids in Woodpark don't like me? What if they're really rough? What if they've got knives and stuff?'

Victoria gave me a quick hug.

'It's not the Wild West,' she said. 'It won't be *that* bad.'

Easy for her to say!

There was another long silence.

'Nice uniform,' said Victoria in the end.

Why did she have to mention the uniform? Didn't she think I felt bad enough already?

I looked down at myself, and tried not to cry.

My new school uniform was totally, totally revolting. The skirt was made of thick scratchy material and the jumper wasn't a whole lot better. Both of them were ugly, ugly bottle-green. Bottle green is a good colour for bottles – for clothes it *so* doesn't work. I thought of my beautiful, well-cut Abbey School uniform, which was squashed up in a box in the garage.

'What's with the shoes?' asked Victoria, looking at the ugly brown things on my feet.

'You've still got hundreds of nice shoes, so why aren't you wearing any of them?'

I sighed.

'None of my nice shoes fit in with the "dress code" of Woodpark School.'

'Woodpark has a dress code?'

I nodded.

'It came in a letter. It goes on for three pages, but it could have been written in one sentence – *if it's nice, you're not allowed to wear it.*'

Victoria laughed.

'And do you know,' I said, warming to my subject. 'There's a banner hanging over the front door of the school, and it says NO FUN ALLOWED HERE!'

'No way!' said Victoria with a horrified gasp.

'Well, actually I haven't been there yet,' I admitted. 'But who knows?'

Victoria laughed again and hugged me.

'I'm glad you've still got your sense of humour,' she said.

I laughed too.

'I think I'm going to need it.'

✫ ♥ ♡

A bit later, Mum and Dad walked me to school.

'Isn't this nice?' said Dad who was still trying

to see the bright side in the disaster that was our lives. 'If I had a job, I wouldn't have time to escort you on your first day in your new school.'

I made a face.

'If you had a job, I wouldn't be going to this stupid school anyway. I'd be on the way to The Abbey, on the bus, on my own.'

'Oh,' said Dad, and we walked the rest of the way in silence.

'Here we are,' said Mum brightly as we stopped outside my new school.

I gulped. I'd never looked closely at this building before. I'd only ever seen it through the tinted windows of Mum's jeep as we drove past on the way to tennis or pony club.

The walls were grey.

The windows were grey.

The bars on the windows were grey.

The sky had even turned grey in sympathy.

Why couldn't I be getting off the bus at The

Abbey, looking forward to hearing about the exotic places my friends had visited over the holidays?

Or why couldn't I be walking along to Victoria's school, looking forward to meeting the friends she'd told me so much about?

Why did I have to be in this grim, grey place?

'Don't make me go in there,' I said. 'It's too scary. Please bring me home.'

Mum shook her head.

'Don't be silly, Eva. You have to go to school.'

I had a brainwave.

'I know. Now that Dad has no job, why doesn't he home-school me? He knows heaps of stuff. He'd be a great teacher.'

'You wouldn't say that if you'd been there when I was learning to drive,' muttered Mum darkly.

Just then three very scary-looking boys went past, pushing and shoving each other as they went through the school gates.

'Did you see them?' I asked when they were safely out of earshot.

Mum put on her bright voice again.

'You shouldn't judge by appearances, Eva. I'm sure they're perfectly nice boys.'

'Why don't I invite them home for tea this evening then?' I said, and watched as Mum's face went pale.

'Come on,' said Dad. 'If we don't go inside you're going to be late.'

I knew there was no point in arguing any more, so I followed my parents, as they led the way into my new school.

☆ ♥ ♡

Mum and Dad shoved me in the door of the principal's office, and after a few polite words, they got to home again.

I wasn't so lucky.

There was no escape for me.

A few minutes later, I was following the principal, Mrs Parker along the corridor. There was a strong smell like old boiled cabbage.

Why couldn't I be back at The Abbey, which smelled of perfume and floor polish?

While we walked, Mrs Parker was muttering about school rules, and locker keys, and fire drills.

I was muttering along in time, like I actually cared.

Why did I need to know all that stuff? This was only a temporary blip. Soon I'd be back in my old school, where I belonged.

At last we stopped at a classroom door.

'Here we are,' said Mrs Parker brightly. 'Sixth Class. After you, my dear.'

She opened the door and pushed me inside. I stood there wishing that the ugly grey floor would swallow me up.

It was weeks since I'd had my nails or my hair done.

I had no make up on. (It was against the dress code of course.)

I was wearing the ugliest clothes I have ever, ever stood up in.

And thirty pairs of eyes were staring at me.

I tried to look like I didn't care.

I tried to think of nice stuff.

I tried to think of Madam Margarita's words.

Help people, and you will get your reward.

How soon could I start helping people?

And how soon would I get out of here?

'Mr Gowing, this is Eva,' said Mrs Parker, after what felt like three hours. 'She's your new student.'

A boy at the back of the class waited until the teachers were looking the other way, and then he flicked a piece of folded paper in my direction. The paper flew into the air and then hit me on the cheek. It really hurt.

I turned to stare at the boy.

Maybe it was time to start helping people.

I'd happily help him to eat his exercise book.

Mr Gowing was talking to me.

'Blah ... Blah ... Welcome ... work hard ... blah, blah and more blah.'

He pointed to an empty chair. There was a boy sitting in the chair next to it.

I was supposed to sit next to a boy?

What if I needed someone to tell me if my hair was OK or if my tights were laddered?

Something told me it was a bit soon to start arguing, so I walked over and sat down.

And so my first day in my new school began.

Chapter Nine

I looked around at the ugly grey walls of the classroom, and felt a sudden pang of sadness as I remembered the wood-panelled walls of The Abbey.

I looked at the sullen-faced boy next to me who smelled of chips, and thought of Emily, who sat next to me at The Abbey. Emily was funny and clever and smelled of violets.

I blinked quickly trying to hold back the tears.

The classroom windows were closed and it was too warm. The sullen-faced boy looked like he was ready to doze off. Outside, the sun had come out. It was shining merrily, taunting us with its freedom. The stiff material of the school uniform was scratching the back of my legs, and my feet were sore from dragging around the ugly, heavy shoes.

I had to escape from this awful place.

And Madam Margarita's plan was the only one I could think of.

❤ ✯ ♡

I should probably explain right now, that I know this whole thing sounds totally stupid.

A few months earlier, if you had told me I'd be visiting a fortune-teller, I wouldn't have believed you.

If you'd told me that I'd believe a fortune-teller, and actually do what she suggested in an effort to change my life, I'd have rolled around the floor and laughed until I was sick.

But a lot had changed in those few months.

And to me, the choice was clear – do what Madam Margarita suggested, or do nothing.

And doing nothing just didn't bear thinking about.

I tried not to think too carefully about how exactly the whole thing was going to work – about how exactly I was going to get my old life back, just by helping other people.

But I'd worry about the details later.

It was time to get started.

☆ ♥ ♡

I looked around the classroom.

Where was the unhappy person who needed my help?

Well, for starters, *I* was unhappy.

But that probably didn't count.

I rested my chin on my hands, and gazed around for a bit. Everyone in the room looked unhappy. But maybe that was only because it was maths class. Even the teacher, scribbling long lines of rubbish on the blackboard, looked like he'd rather be somewhere, anywhere else.

Mr Gowing was explaining a maths problem, and telling us about some boring old Ancient

Greek maths guy. I'd already done the same problem in my old school. I hadn't found it fun first time round, so how exactly was it supposed to have improved in the months since then?

Half way through the maths class, I found someone who definitely needed some help.

'Yesss,' I whispered to myself.

The boy beside me woke up and stared at me like I was an idiot.

'*Yesss*, I really love maths,' I whispered, and he looked at me like I was an even bigger idiot.

As soon as the boy was busy gouging another hole in the desk with his compass, I took a closer look at the lucky girl – the first person in my 'help people and get out of here' project.

She was small and pretty, and she was sitting right at the front of the class. Her name was Petronella (which, on its own, was a good enough reason to be unhappy, I thought).

The other reason was that the teacher kept

picking on her. Whenever she even whispered to the girl next to her, Mr Gowing shouted at her to be quiet – like whispering was this huge crime – and like the rest of the class wasn't whispering madly whenever he turned to face the blackboard.

And the worst thing was, no matter what Mr Gowing said, Petronella never even blinked. It was almost like she was so used to being picked on, that she didn't care any more.

The lesson dragged on and on and on. Soon I knew far more than I ever wanted to know about geometry.

I looked around and all I could see were glazed eyes and bored faces – it was like I'd dropped into the set of a very bad zombie movie.

Suddenly Petronella dropped her book to the ground with a clatter. I jumped and a few of the boys laughed.

Mr Gowing spun on his heel.

'Petronella,' he said crossly. 'I think you did that deliberately, just to annoy me.'

For once, Petronella reacted.

'That's not fair,' she said. 'It was an accident.'

Mr Gowing walked to her desk and leaned down towards her with a mean look on his face.

'So, Petronella,' he hissed. 'So I'm not being fair. And what are you going to do about it – run home and tell your mama?'

There were a few sniggers from the back of the class.

How could anyone find this funny?

What kind of a sick school had I ended up in?

Petronella took a deep breath.

'Actually, I think I will tell my mother,' she said.

Now Mr Gowing gave a laugh.

'Ha,' he said. 'Promises, promises. I know you'll never tell on me. You're just too chicken.'

Petronella didn't reply. I looked around in

horror. Some of the kids were giggling. Even worse, some looked totally bored, like this kind of thing happened every day.

I made up my mind.

Mr Gowing mustn't be allowed to treat the poor girl like that.

It just wasn't right.

All I had to do was figure out a way to help her.

There's an ad on TV that says if you see someone being bullied at school, then you should talk to your teacher.

But what were you supposed to do if the bully *was* your teacher?

I had to talk to Petronella.

I had to help her to be strong.

I had to persuade her to talk to her mother about the way Mr Gowing was bullying her.

Or maybe she should go to the principal?

Perhaps there was a board of governers that should know?

I turned to the back page of my maths book and started to make notes.

Chapter Ten

After what felt like a hundred years, maths class was over.

After what felt like a thousand years, the school day was over too.

A bell rang, and everyone jumped up and started to shove their books into their bags.

A couple of girls came over to chat to me. It was nice of them, but I didn't really want to get involved.

What was the point of making friends here if I was going back to my old school before long?

So I smiled at them and said I had to rush, and they smiled back and said, 'See you tomorrow.'

I hoped I wouldn't be spending too many

tomorrows in this dump.

And then I raced off after Petronella.

☆ ♥ ♡

It took me ages to catch her. She was walking along the road with two other girls. I was glad she had friends. But then, what kind of friends just stand by and watch their friend being bullied?

I walked up to the three girls, trying to look all relaxed and casual, and not like I could barely breathe from running so fast.

'Hi,' I said.

'Hi,' they said back.

Then they kept walking.

I realised that maybe I should have planned my attack a bit better. Too late now though.

'Er, Petronella, there's something I'd like to talk to you about,' I said.

'So talk,' she said.

This was totally embarrassing. I hopped from one foot to another. The clump-clump of my heavy shoes on the footpath made me sound like an elephant tap-dancing.

'It's ...... it's kind of private.'

Now Petronella looked at me like I was crazy. I couldn't really blame her. I'd never in my life spoken to this girl, and all of a sudden I wanted to have a private conversation with her. She probably thought I was some weird kind of stalker.

Her friends giggled.

'Do you want some quiet time with your new friend?' asked one.

She shrugged.

'Whatever. I'll catch up with you as soon as ...'

I could have finished her sentence for her – *I'll catch up with you as soon as I manage to shake off this loser.*

But luckily she was too kind to say this.

'I'll catch up with you in a minute,' she said.

The two girls waved goodbye, and walked a

small bit ahead, staying close enough to rescue Petronella if things started to turn nasty.

Petronella turned to me.

'So, Eva, what's so urgent and so private?' she asked, but not in a mean way. She even gave me an encouraging smile, like she thought there was an outside chance that she might actually be interested in what I had to say.

Suddenly I realised that she really was a nice girl, and that made me even more determined to help her.

'It's about the teacher – Mr Gowing,' I said.

A small smile came over Petronella's face.

I wondered why she was smiling.

Maybe because she wouldn't have to see Mr Gowing for another twenty hours or so?

'What about Mr Gowing?' she asked.

I was starting to feel a bit stupid, so I spoke in a rush. 'He treats you differently to everyone else,' I said. 'He gives you a hard time over stuff he lets the other kids away with. It's so not fair. That man shouldn't be allowed to behave like that. You should go ahead and do what you threatened. You should tell your mother.'

She shrugged, still with that funny half-smile on her face.

'I did tell my mum once. But she only laughed. She says it's exactly what I deserve.'

I was so surprised that at first I couldn't speak.

Clearly things were worse than I had feared.

What kind of mother would laugh when she hears that her daughter is being bullied by a teacher?

I stopped walking and tried to gather my thoughts.

Petronella stopped too, and we looked at each other.

'Petronella, this is very serious,' I said. 'Something will have to be done.'

Petronella still had that strange smile on her

face and it was starting to make me a bit nervous. Maybe all this bullying had made her go slightly crazy.

She looked at her watch.

'Thanks for your concern, Eva,' she said. 'But if I don't go now, I'm going to be late for hockey practice. I'll arrange a meeting between my mum and … Mr Gowing, OK?'

I nodded happily.

'OK. I suppose that's a start. But you need a definite plan. Where and when do you think the meeting can happen?'

She grinned.

'Oh, I suppose they could meet around the kitchen table at my place – probably at about six o'clock this evening.'

What was she on about?

Maybe this girl truly was crazy, and I shouldn't have got involved.

Maybe her problems were the kind that I

couldn't possibly help her with.

Suddenly Petronella gave me a big hug.

I backed away as soon as I could.

If this girl was crazy, I totally didn't like being hugged by her.

I totally, totally didn't like being hugged by her in a public place.

'Thanks, Eva,' she said. 'Thanks for being worried about me. It's really nice of you to try to help me. But, you see, Mr Gowing is .... my dad!'

'Mr Gowing is your *dad*?' I repeated stupidly.

She nodded.

'I'm afraid so. He's not bullying me when he says that stuff in class. He's just having a laugh. It's stupid I know, but it's kind of like a joke between us. It's not a big deal.'

'So all the other kids were laughing because they were in on the joke?'

She nodded.

'And Mr Gowing *wasn't* being a bully, he was just being a normal dad – totally embarrassing?'

She nodded again.

I slapped my forehead.

'You must think I'm an idiot.'

She smiled.

'No, you're not. It was very nice of you to try and help me. So thank you. And now I've really got to go. I'll see you tomorrow, and maybe you can come and sit next to me and my friends.'

'Do you think Mr Gowing would let me change places?'

She laughed.

'I think I might be able to sort that one out.'

I laughed too.

'Oh, and one more thing,' she said. 'Call me Ella. Everyone does – except for my dad – and he only uses my full name because he knows it annoys me.'

She gave me another hug, and then she ran on

to catch up with her friends.

And I walked slowly home.

☆ ♥ ♡

Victoria phoned that night, and I told her all about my new school.

'So no knives and no guns and no cat-fights?' she said. 'Sounds totally boring to me.'

Then I told her about Ella, and how I had tried to help her.

'That was so nice of you,' she said – when she'd finally stopped laughing. 'Imagine trying so hard to help someone on your very first day.'

I didn't answer. I felt bad that Victoria thought I was being nice for the sake of being nice. I'd sort of neglected to mention Madam Margarita's part in the whole story.

'Do you think you and Ella might become friends?' asked Victoria then.

'Are you getting jealous,' I shot back, before remembering that Victoria is far too generous to ever feel jealous of anyone.

'No,' she said. 'I'd just like you to have a friend in your new school, that's all. And Ella sounds nice.'

'You mean nicer than my friends from The Abbey?'

Now it was Victoria's turn to hesitate. She had never much liked my friends from my old school. She said they weren't interested in people, that they were only interested in fancy cars and exotic holidays. (Although, when she turned out to be right, and they all managed to forget me overnight, she was kind enough not to mention it.)

Even though Victoria wasn't giving me a hard time, I felt a sudden need to defend my old school.

'You know, there were nearly two hundred girls in The Abbey,' I said. 'And they weren't all mean.'

'Just the ones you chose for your friends?'

I thought about arguing but then didn't bother. I knew Victoria was right. I *had* chosen my friends badly. When the going got tough, they got going – right out of my life.

'Sorry,' said Victoria. 'I shouldn't have put it like that. Forget them, Eva. You're better than the whole lot of them put together.'

'Anyway,' I said, changing the subject quickly. 'I have heaps of history homework.'

And we talked about totally boring schoolwork until Mum called me for my tea.

Chapter Eleven

As I walked to school the next day, stomping along in my heavy brown shoes, I made up my mind that I'd just have to try harder. I had let a whole day go by without actually managing to help anyone. If I continued like that I'd never get my old life back.

I hadn't really believed Madam Margarita when she said it wasn't going to be easy – and that was sure turning out to be a mistake.

When I got to my classroom, Ella called me over. 'You can sit here, Eva,' she said. 'With Chloe and Amy and me. It's all sorted with Da— I mean Mr Gowing.'

I smiled.

'Thanks.'

I still didn't plan on staying in that dump of a school for long, but while I was there. I figured I might as well make the most of it.

✯ ♥ ♡

I'd decided to spend the day watching the other kids in the class. There were thirty of them – surely one of them would need some help.

Surely one of them would be my passport out of there.

Soon though, I discovered that lots of the kids needed help – but none of them needed help in a way that I could do anything about.

How could I help the boy called Joshua who kept tearing pieces of paper from his school-books and flicking them around the room?

How could I help Shannon, the girl who sat in the middle of the room with a huge smile on her face, even though she didn't seem to understand a single word that any of the teachers said?

Then I started to pay more attention to the classroom assistant.

Her name was Dawn, and she walked around the classroom like there was a huge, heavy rock on her shoulders. She looked like the tiniest thing would prompt her to lie down in a corner crying buckets of tears.

But the more I watched this sad woman, the happier I felt.

Dawn was perfect.

All I had to do was find out why she was so sad, and then I could go ahead and fix it.

✩ ❤ ♡

Dawn left the building as soon as school was over, and I watched as she took the road towards town. I said hurried good-byes to my new friends, and raced after Dawn.

I ran down the street and quickly spotted her. It wasn't difficult. She was marching along so fiercely that the crowds were parting to let her through. I raced into the space behind her, and followed.

Soon we came to a coffee shop. Dawn went inside, and joined another woman at a table. She waved at a waitress and ordered a coffee. I sat at a table nearby. I hoped no one was going to ask me to buy something as I had the big total of five cents in my pocket. I pulled out a geography book, and pretended to be totally interested in a map of France.

Dawn was stirring her coffee like she wanted to make a hole in the bottom of the cup.

'Did you tell her?' asked her friend.

Dawn shook her head.

'I can't do it. I can't go.'

The friend gave a big long sigh.

'Just make your mind up. Tell her. Tell her you're going on a holiday with Julie and me.'

Dawn interrupted her, 'But it's not just a holiday. It's not a week at the beach or a few days up a mountain. It's two whole months. In South America.'

The friend smiled and rubbed her hands together.

'I know. I can still hardly believe it's going to happen. Now you just need to tell your mother and then we can get on with it. And then, after the trip, your mother will be used to you being away, and you'll be able to live with Julie and me. We'll find a place big enough for the three of us, and it'll be the beginning of the rest of our lives.'

For one second Dawn's eyes lit up, and then the light faded like a match-flame in the wind.

'I would love that so much,' she said, 'but I can't do it,' she said. 'Since Dad died, Mum has no one else. I *want* to do all this stuff with you and Julie, but I can't. Mum needs me.'

The friend was cross. She stood up.

'You're sad all the time, Dawn. It's not right. It's time you started to live your own life,' she said. 'Anyway, Julie and I are going to the travel agents to book our flights tomorrow afternoon. Call one of us before then if you change your mind.'

Then without another word, she left the coffee shop.

Dawn sat there, stirring her coffee even more furiously than before.

I sighed.

Poor Dawn. No wonder she was such a misery. She deserved to have a life away from her mother.

Maybe I could help her?

Was there a way I could persuade her to go away with her friends?

But what about her poor, lonely mother?

What good would it be if I made Dawn happy, but at the same time, ruined her mother's life?

This helping stuff was turning out to be very complicated.

Soon afterwards, Dawn stood up and walked out, trailing her sadness behind her like a dark cloud. I followed her, because I couldn't think of anything else to do.

Luckily Dawn was too caught up in her own thoughts to notice that she had just acquired a new shadow.

Soon Dawn stopped at a house. She unlocked the door and let herself in.

'I'm home, Mum,' I heard her say.

'I'm on the phone to your Aunt Hannah,' came a voice from an open window at the side of the house. 'Make yourself a cup of tea and I'll be there in a minute.'

I walked around to the side of the house and sat on the grass under the open window. I know that eavesdropping isn't a very nice habit, but I couldn't stop myself. I had to learn more about Dawn and her mother.

Was there a way that I could help the two of them?

Was there a way that they could both be happy?

'Dawn's home,' came her mother's voice through the open window. Then there was a long sigh. 'I'm sorry, Hannah,' she said. 'I know your plan makes perfect sense. I know that you and Mary need to buy a new apartment. I know that we could buy a three-bedroomed place between us. I know we could have a wonderful life together – the three Brady sisters back together at last. But who would take care of Dawn? She needs me. I'm all she has. Since her dad died, she's been very down in the dumps. She never even goes out with her friends any more ... Now I have to go and make her something to eat. The poor child must be starving.'

She hesitated while the person on the other end of the line said something, and then she sighed again.

'Yes, I know Mary will be disappointed. Tell

her she can give me a call in ten minutes. I'll explain everything to her then.'

I heard the click as the phone was hung up. I lay down on the warm grass and smiled. Dawn was unhappy because she thought her mother needed her, and her mother was unhappy because she thought Dawn needed her. And all they both wanted to do was to get on with their lives.

All I had to do was let each one know what the other one was feeling.

But how on earth was I going to do that?

Chapter Twelve

Five minutes later I had a plan. I'm not sure if it was a great plan, but it was the best I could come up with in such a short time.

I pulled my phone out of my schoolbag, ran up to the door of Dawn's house, and knocked hard. Dawn opened the door and stood there under her own personal black cloud.

'Oh,' I said. 'I didn't know you lived here. What a coincidence.'

She stared at me for a minute.

'You're the new girl in school,' she said. 'Eva, isn't it?'

I nodded.

'What are you doing here?' she asked.

I smiled my best smile.

'It's about the project Mr Gowing set us,' I said, hoping that Dawn wouldn't remember that he hadn't mentioned a project. 'It's a science project,' I added. 'Science is my favourite subject.'

'And?'

'And I'm going to do my project on butterflies, and while I was walking past your house just now, I saw the coolest butterfly fly into your garden. I need to take a picture of it. Can I go look for it?'

I helpfully held up my phone. (It was ancient – at least six months old, but at least it had a camera.)

Dawn shrugged.

'Sure, just don't trample on the flowers.'

I didn't move.

'Er ...... actually, I need your help. I need you to sit with me and rustle the flowers, so that the butterfly will fly out. Then I can take the picture.'

I didn't wait for an answer. I walked over to the flowers under the open window, and I sat down. I smiled to myself as Dawn followed me and sat down next to me. Dawn smiled too. She looked younger and prettier when she smiled.

I wondered if I could help her to smile a lot more.

'We need to be very quiet, so we won't frighten the butterfly,' I whispered.

Dawn nodded, and then I continued.

'Now, what I need you to do is to shake each flower one by one, very gently.'

Dawn smiled again.

'I think I can manage that,' she whispered, and gently shook the first flower.

We sat there for a while. It was peaceful, in a weird kind of way. Dawn shook each flower one by one, and when she had shaken them all, I had to pretend to be surprised that the non-existent butterfly hadn't flown out.

Now what was I going to do?

Why wasn't the phone inside the house ringing?

'I'm sorry, Eva,' said Dawn, starting to get up. 'We must have missed it. It must have flown away while you were knocking on the door.'

I grabbed her arm and pulled her down again.

Was I going to have to sit on her to get her to stay there?

'Please,' I whispered. 'Wait another few minutes. Maybe the butterfly will come back.'

I knew this was really pathetic, and probably Dawn did too, but she smiled kindly.

'OK,' she said. 'Since it seems to mean so much to you, I'll wait another few minutes.'

Just then the phone inside the house rang. I could hear footsteps as Dawn's mother went to answer it.

'We need to be very quiet,' I whispered to Dawn. 'Or the butterfly won't come back.'

Then I sat there and listened to one half of Dawn's mother's telephone conversation.

'Hi, Mary. Thanks for ringing me. And thanks for inviting me to live with you and Hannah, but I have to say no .... Yes, I know I'm throwing away a great opportunity.......................'

Then there was a long gap. I sneaked a quick look at Dawn. She didn't say anything, but I knew that she was listening to her mother too.

Her mother spoke again, sounding really sad.

'Yes, Mary, I know all of that. I've been over and over it with Hannah already. It would be absolutely perfect for me. But the problem is Dawn. She has no one else to take care of her. What would she do if I suddenly announced that I was going to live with you and Hannah? I'm sorry, but I just couldn't do that to the child.'

Child! Dawn had to be at least twenty-five years old.

Beside me, I could hear Dawn's breathing change, like she was really tense or afraid ...... or excited.

The phone conversation was over seconds later.

'Goodbye, Mary, and thanks anyway,' said Dawn's mother sadly. 'I hope you and Hannah have fun when you go apartment-hunting tomorrow.'

Then I heard a dull click as the phone was put down.

Dawn jumped up, looking all flushed and happy.

'I'm sorry, Eva,' she said. 'I've got to go inside to talk to my mother. It's an emergency.'

'Whatever,' I said, trying not to look as happy as I felt.

Dawn ran to the front door, and then ran back to me.

'I'm sorry about your butterfly,' she said. 'I'll

look for some pictures on the internet later on if you like.'

I shook my head.

'It's OK, thanks. I've changed my mind. I think I'll do my project on worms instead. They're easier to take pictures of. Now you go ahead and talk to your mother. I'm sure you've got lots to say to her.'

Dawn gave me a funny look, and then ran inside.

I stood up, brushed the grass off my ugly green uniform and set off for home.

Result.

✯ ♥ ♡

The next morning, Dawn practically skipped into the classroom. She was smiling so much that she looked like her face was going to crack in two. Several times I could hear her humming happily.

At break time, I overheard her talking to one of

the other classroom assistants. Dawn was so excited she could hardly get the words out properly.

'... and everything is slipping perfectly into place,' she said. 'By the time we get back from South America, Mum will have moved in with her sisters and my two friends and I are going to move into Mum's house. Mum said we can redecorate if we want. We're going to ......'

I didn't wait to hear any more, and I walked away to look for Ella and Amy and Chloe.

I was very glad for Dawn, but I couldn't help feeling sorry for myself.

When was my life going to change?

When was I going to get my happy ending?

Chapter Thirteen

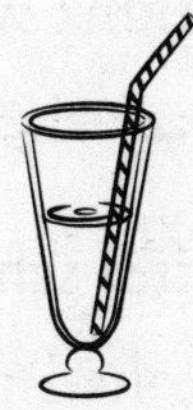

The rest of that week passed very slowly. Whenever I got really fed up, I tried to remember Madam Margarita's words.

Help people.

Help people.

It was like an echo rattling round inside my brain.

Soon I was blue in the face from holding doors open for people, and from helping little old ladies across the street.

But still nothing changed.

Friday rolled around again and I was still a pupil in Woodpark School.

I was still living in a horrible house.

Dad still didn't have a job or a car.

I was still where I didn't want to be.

✯ ❤ ♡

Victoria called over after school on Friday.

To get upstairs, we had to climb over Dad, who was lying there repairing one of the broken steps.

'Sorry, girls,' he said. 'Just trying to patch the place up a bit.'

I giggled. Now that Dad wasn't working, he was totally bored, and he was driving Mum crazy. Every time she turned around he was whacking something with a hammer or attacking something with a screwdriver. Mum said she was afraid to sit down in case he tried to saw her in half.

Victoria looked around approvingly.

'The house is looking lovely,' she said to my dad. 'You've got a talent for home-improvement.'

I wondered how Dad would take that. Up to recently he'd had a talent for running one of the biggest businesses in town.

But Dad looked at Victoria like she was his best friend in the whole world.

'Thanks,' he said, beaming so much that he accidentally thumped his finger with the hammer.

Victoria and I giggled, and ran upstairs.

✯ ❤ ♡

'You look really nice, Victoria,' I said as we sat on the tiny bed in my tiny bedroom.

She didn't argue, probably because she knew I was right. She was wearing a beautiful new top and new jeans, and her brown hair had the coolest touches of gold running through it.

I was wearing clothes that I'd had forever, and my highlights were almost completely grown out.

I couldn't stop myself from leaning over and

touching the soft fabric of her top.

'You can borrow it any time you like,' she said.

I nodded, afraid that if I tried to speak, I might cry instead.

I was always the one who had the nicest things.

I was always the one who lent Victoria stuff.

That's just the way it was meant to be.

I looked around my bedroom. I had done my best, by putting up posters and stuff, but nothing could change the fact that it was a very small and very ugly room. The walls were painted a dark muddy-brown colour, and the carpet looked like it had seen better days – hundreds of years ago. I had planned to ask Dad to paint the walls, but when I said that to Mum, she hesitated, and I figured that she didn't want to spend any of our precious money on paint.

Suddenly I couldn't bear to sit there for another second.

'Come on,' I said, grabbing my jacket and

heading for the door.

'Where are we going?' asked Victoria.

I shrugged.

'I don't know yet. Just out of here.'

We walked to the park, but there was a gang of scary-looking boys there, so we didn't stay.

'We could go to the cinema,' suggested Victoria.

'No,' I said quickly.

I didn't have the money for the cinema. I didn't have the money to do anything fun. I thought sadly of how things used to be. In my old house, the table next to my bed was always strewn with coins and notes that I'd carelessly emptied from my pockets. Now I never got pocket money any more, and when I needed money for school, Mum doled it out like she was giving me the last of her life's savings.

Sometimes I was afraid that she truly was giving me the last of her life's savings.

Victoria hesitated.

'I can lend you the money if you like.'

'No,' I said even more quickly. I knew Victoria was being kind, and I would really have loved to go to the cinema, but there was no way I was borrowing money from her.

How could I, when I had no idea when I was ever going to be able to pay her back?

I sighed.

'I don't mind if you want to go home,' I said. 'Or maybe one of your other friends would like to go to the cinema with you.'

She shook her head.

'Stop being an idiot,' she said. 'It's you I want to hang out with. We'll find something to do that doesn't cost money.'

In the end, we went to a chemist's shop near Victoria's house. Victoria's sister's friend, Bethany, was working there, and she let us try on all the make-up. I had so much fun trying on all the different lip-glosses that I forgot to be upset that I couldn't afford to buy any of them.

After a while, Bethany made us wipe our faces clean.

'I'll do you up properly,' she said. 'I need to practice for my night class. The theme this week is "Dramatic Looks."'

Much later, Victoria and I fell around laughing as we left the shop.

'That's the best fun I've had in ages,' I said. 'But you look like you've been in an accident.'

'Well, you look like there's been an explosion in the blusher factory,' she retorted.

'I think poor Bethany needs a bit more practice,' I said, and then we laughed some more, as we headed towards home.

☆ ♥ ♡

We hadn't gone far, when I saw a familiar figure wheeling herself along a side street. She wasn't wearing her shiny turban or her sparkly shawl, but I knew straight away who it was.

'Can you hang on a sec?' I said to Victoria. 'I need to talk to that woman.'

Victoria shrugged.

'Who is she?'

I was glad that Victoria hadn't seen Madam Margarita the time before, and now I certainly didn't plan on explaining who she was.

'Oh, it's just someone I know,' I said. 'I'll only be a minute.'

I ran up to Madam Margarita. She looked surprised to see me.

'Oh, it's the Princess,' she said, but not unkindly.

I didn't answer. She had never looked very mysterious, but now she looked nothing at all like a fortune-teller.

She just looked very cold and very tired.

'Nice make-up,' she said.

I put my hand to my face in embarrassment.

‘I’d forgotten about that,’ I said. ‘You see—’

Madam Margarita put her hand up to stop me.

‘You don’t always have to explain yourself to me,’ she said. ‘Don’t apologise for being young and exuberant.’

‘Er … can I ask you something?’ I said.

She shrugged her thin shoulders.

‘It’s a free country.’

‘Remember what you said, about helping people?’

She didn’t answer, so I continued.

‘Well, I did it. I did what you said. I’ve helped loads and loads of people.’

‘I see you’ve been helping pre-schoolers with their spatter-painting classes.’

‘What …? I began before I realised that she was talking about my make-up.

‘Ha ha, very funny. Not.’

‘Sorry,’ she said, smiling. ‘I couldn’t resist.

Anyway, you were saying?'

'I've helped loads of people,' I said again. 'But it didn't work. Nothing has changed.'

Madam Margarita raised one eyebrow.

'Maybe things have changed for the people you helped, though.'

'I don't care about the other people....' She raised the other eyebrow and I corrected myself. 'Well, I do care about them, and there's this one woman, Dawn, I totally turned her life around ... but I care about me too. Why can't I be happy?'

She smiled.

'You seem like a nice girl – underneath it all. I'm sure things will turn out OK for you in the end. Keep on helping others and you won't go far wrong. Just remember, nothing changes quickly. You have to be patient.'

'Patience is for losers,' I muttered.

Madam Margarita laughed a big happy laugh.

'That's funny,' she said.

I looked at her in surprise. If I was as poor as she seemed to be, and if I had to use a wheelchair, would I ever think anything was funny again?

Would I ever be able to laugh?

Would I ever even be able to smile?

'I'd better get back to my friend.' I said.

'OK,' said Madam Margarita. 'But there's one more thing.'

'What?'

'That'll be another ten euro.'

I gulped.

'But I don't have.......' I began.

Madam Margarita gave another happy laugh.

'I'm joking,' she said. 'Now off you go and have a nice day.'

I smiled as she wheeled herself away, on perfectly silent, squeak-free wheels.

Chapter Fourteen

On Monday, Ella wasn't at school, and I ended up sitting next to a girl who I'd never noticed before. She was tall and thin, and her straight brown hair hung like a curtain half way across her face. What I could see of her face was blank, like it had been drawn by an artist who wasn't very good at catching expressions, She sat still and silent in her seat, almost like she wanted to be invisible.

'I'm Eva,' I said as I sat down.

'I know,' said the girl. Her voice was hoarse, almost like she wasn't used to talking.

Then there was a long silence.

'And?' I said.

'And what?'

I sighed.

'This is the bit where you say, *Hi, Eva, my name is whatever. Nice to meet you!* and all that stuff. You know – it's called conversation. Lots of people do it. You should try it some time.'

It was hard to tell from behind her curtain of hair, but I don't think she even smiled.

'I'm Ruby,' she said, and then she hunched over her homework diary, making it clear that this very short conversation was now over.

I was considering getting up and finding somewhere else to sit, but just then Mr Gowing came in to the classroom, so reluctantly, I stayed where I was.

It was a very long day.

After another few attempts, I stopped trying to chat to Ruby. I felt like I was wasting my breath. It would have been easier to talk to one of the grey classroom walls.

When at last the bell rang for home time, I hurried to pack up my books.

'Bye, Ruby,' I said. 'It was totally fun chatting to you today.'

She gazed at me with the same blank expression she'd worn all day.

No conversation skills and no sense of humour I thought. I really know how to pick people to sit next to.

Ruby was still gazing at me.

'Be like that,' I muttered as I zipped up my bag.

But then I sighed as Madam Margarita's words began their daily echo through my head.

Help people.

Any fool could see that Ruby needed help, but needing help and wanting help were two very different things.

And besides, how could you help someone who wouldn't even talk to you?

But …

'Hey, Ruby,' I said. 'Do you want to be my partner for our maths project? We could go to the library after school tomorrow and get started if you like.'

Ruby put her head up quickly and her hair swished back. For the first time, I saw her face properly. She had perfect, clear skin and huge brown eyes. For one second, the blank expression disappeared, and she looked … surprised? …… pleased? I wasn't sure which.

'Thank you, Eva,' she said quietly.

'So you want us to work together?' I said, realising that I had been half-hoping that she was going to refuse.

'No,' she said quickly. 'But thank you for asking me anyway.'

Suddenly I felt offended.

'So why don't you want to work with me?' I asked.

It's not like people are queuing up to be your partner.

'I'm going to do my maths project on my own. Mr Gowing said that's OK.'

Why would anyone choose to work on their own, when they could be working with a friend who'd do at least half the work?

It was like Ruby could read my mind.

'I'm sorry, Eva,' she said. 'I don't mean to be rude, but ... I'm a very busy person ... I don't really have time for friends. Don't take it personally, OK?'

That was just about the weirdest thing anyone had ever said to me.

How could anyone be too busy for friends?

Ruby must have some very time-consuming hobbies.

While I was still thinking of a reply, Ruby had picked up her bag and was gone.

The next day I sat next to Ella again, and we

did our project together.

And so another week passed by in a flurry of small acts of kindness that didn't seem to be getting me anywhere closer to my dream.

Chapter Fifteen

On Saturday morning, Mum handed me five euro. Before I could get excited, she said,

'Go to the market in Bridge Street, and buy me some apples and bananas.'

I gasped like she'd asked me to go to the moon.

'The market?' I repeated. 'What's wrong with Johann? Is he sick?'

(Johann was the man who delivered a big box of organic fruit and vegetables to our house every week. He was really nice, and in the summer, he always brought extra strawberries because he knew I loved them.)

Mum sat down, and I braced myself for a speech.

'Darling, you do understand how bad things are financially?'

Why would I understand?

She'd only told me about ten thousand times?

'But you said we had to cut out luxuries,' I protested. 'And I'm OK with that – well not OK exactly, but at least I understand where you're coming from. But surely fruit isn't a luxury?'

Mum gave a sad smile.

'Welcome to the real world, darling. In the real world, not everyone gets their fruit delivered by a nice Dutch man in a pretty green van with flowers painted on the side. And I'm afraid we can't afford it any more either.'

'But the market?' I said again. 'Why can't I go to the supermarket, where normal people shop?'

She sighed.

'Even in the supermarket, fruit is expensive. And Gemma next door shops in the market all the time. She tells me that fruit there is a lot cheaper, and it's lovely and fresh too.'

I knew there wasn't any point in arguing. My mum, who never used to mind spending hundreds of euro on a handbag, was becoming an expert on saving a few cents here and there.

So, feeling a bit like Little Red Riding Hood, I set off for the market, hoping with all my heart that I wouldn't meet any wolves on the way.

✯ ♥ ♡

It was a lovely sunny day, and the market was crowded. Everyone seemed happy as they wandered by, laden with bunches of flowers and newspaper-wrapped parcels. After a while, I found a stall selling fruit and vegetables. There were crowds of people waiting to buy.

'Why is it so slow?' asked a big wide man who was standing in front of me.

'It's always like this,' said the woman next to him. 'The poor girl who is running the stall is on her own. I don't know how she manages.'

Who cared about the stall-holder?

How was I supposed to manage?

I'd never bought stuff that wasn't already packed up in plastic bags with labels on them.

How was I supposed to figure out how much fruit I could buy with my five euro?

Should I keep buying one apple and one banana at a time until my money ran out?

And how popular would that make me with the people behind me in the queue?

While I was still trying to decide what to do, the big man in front of me moved away, and I found myself standing right at the front of the fruit stall. The sun was shining in my eyes, and I blinked to make sure that I was seeing correctly. After a few blinks I was sure – I'd know that long brown hair anywhere – I'd know that blank expression anywhere – the girl serving the fruit and vegetables was Ruby.

She didn't see me. She was working as fast as

she possibly could – weighing stuff, and taking money and giving change and shoving fruit and vegetables into big brown paper bags.

She looked pale and tired and stressed. Even though this girl was totally weird, and totally unfriendly, it was impossible not to feel sorry for her.

'Would you like me to help you for a while?' I said, but Ruby didn't hear me as a rough woman was shouting at her to hurry up and weigh her potatoes.

'Would ...?' I began again, but then I stopped.

I knew I was wasting my breath.

I knew that offering to help Ruby was a mistake.

I knew she'd just say no.

She'd just blank me, like she had at school.

She looked like a girl who'd already had lots of practice at blanking people.

So I wriggled out from the crowd of

customers, and slipped behind the stall. When Ruby reached for a bag to put the potatoes into, I was ready, with an open bag in my hand.

For one second she stared at me, and then she took the bag, filled it with potatoes and handed it to the customer.

'Thanks,' she muttered, and I smiled to myself.

Progress.

The next customer selected some apples, handed them to me, and I put them in a bag, while Ruby sorted out the money.

Ruby still looked a bit confused, but the customers had copped on fairly quickly.

The two of us worked really quickly, and after ten minutes, the crowd had cleared and we had a chance to breathe.

'You can go now,' said Ruby, as she rearranged some apples that had slipped into the pear section of the stall.

'But I was just starting to enjoy myself. And besides, it's sure to get busy again in a few minutes.'

She looked embarrassed.

'I'll manage. I'm used to it. I've been doing this for ... well for a long time.'

I still didn't move.

'Thanks for helping me, Eva,' said Ruby. 'But I can't afford to pay you or anything.'

'I'm just helping you, 'I said. 'I don't expect to be paid.'

Now Ruby looked even more puzzled. 'Why would you want to help me?'

I didn't answer at first. There was no way I was telling this girl about Madam Margarita.

Clearly she was already a fully signed-up weirdo, and I didn't want her thinking that she and I had something in common.

'I just like helping people,' I said. 'Now get ready, I can see some customers coming.'

☆ ♥ ♡

The morning passed quickly. Some of the customers were really nice. Some were funny. And some were just plain weird.

At one stage a tiny woman hobbled over towards the stall. She looked like she was about two hundred years old, with a wizened face and long straggly hair. She was wearing a brown coat that was patched here and there with scraps of grey fabric that looked suspiciously like cut up underpants. On her feet was a pair of old mens' working boots.

'The poor little thing,' I whispered as she came closer.

'Poor my eye,' whispered Ruby back. 'That's Mamie. Everyone in the market hates her. She's one of the richest women in town, but she's totally mean. She's never once paid full price for anything here.'

I grinned.

'Leave her to me. I like a challenge.'

Soon, the woman was next to us, picking through the apples.

'How much are these?' she asked in a croaky voice, exactly like the wicked witch in a fairy-tale. I wondered if she planned to poison one of the apples and feed it to some unsuspecting young girl.

'Same as last week,' said Ruby. 'Six for a euro.'

'Six for a euro!' said Mamie with a loud cackle that made everyone around turn and stare at us. A few of the nearby stallholders gave sympathetic looks in our direction.

'That's daylight robbery,' she said. 'They're all bruised. Look.'

She held up two perfect, unblemished apples.

Ruby went red.

'Maybe we can....' she began, but I edged her aside.

'No, Ruby,' I said. 'You've made a mistake.

These aren't six for a euro, remember? These are the specially imported Guatamalan Gold apples. There's only a few left and they're two for a euro.'

Mamie narrowed her beady eyes and licked her dry, cracked lips.

'You said six for a euro, so you have to sell them to me for that. It's the law. I know my rights.'

'I bet you do,' I muttered.

Then I gave a big long sigh.

'I suppose she's right,' I said to Ruby. 'We'll have to give her six for a euro. But don't make that mistake again, or you'll have us bankrupt in no time.'

I packed up six apples, managing to sneak in one bruised one that had been put aside for pig-food. Ruby took the euro from Mamie's stick-like hand, and Mamie scuttled off, cackling as she went.

'Old Mamie's too cute for the lot of them.'

There was a sudden clapping sound. I looked

up to see that the stallholders on either side were applauding me. I gave a small bow, trying to hide the red that was spreading across my cheeks.

This was so much fun.

☆ ♥ ♡

An hour later, the market closed for the day. By then I was exhausted.

Who'd have thought that selling fruit and vegetables could be so tiring?

'What time did you start this morning?' I asked.

'Seven-thirty,' said Ruby.

I gulped. Even on school mornings I didn't get up that early.

'And do you work here every Saturday?'

She nodded.

'Yes. And on Sundays too, and on Wednesday and Friday afternoons after school.'

'Wow,' I said.

No wonder the poor girl had no time for

friends. I was having trouble understanding how she found time for basic stuff like sleeping and eating.

It was all too hard for me to take in. Victoria's big sister babysat occasionally, but I'd never before met someone my age who had a real job.

'But . . .' I struggled, but I couldn't find a polite way to ask the question. So I went right ahead and asked it the rude way. 'Aren't there laws about young people like us working for a living?'

'There are laws about young people like us starving too,' snapped Ruby.

'Sorry,' I said. 'I didn't mean to offend you. It's just . . . . . . well you're running a market stall – all on your own.'

She shrugged.

'It's really my mum's stall, but she's been sick lately, so I have to do it. My uncle opens up the stall for me and he lifts all the heavy boxes, and my big sister helps out whenever she's not working. It's not so bad really.'

She stopped speaking and her face went blank again. She had only spoken a few sentences, but she looked like she was sorry she had said so much.

We didn't speak any more, as I helped her to carry the half-empty boxes into a shed behind the stall. Ruby was just locking up when I remembered why I was in the market in the first place.

What was Mum going to say when I got back, having spent two hours in the market buying nothing?

I pulled the five euro note from my pocket.

'How many apples and bananas can I buy with this?'

Ruby didn't answer. She took the money from me, and slipped it into her pocket. Then she pulled a huge paper bag from the pile. She filled it with apples, bananas, pears and oranges. After the morning I'd just spent, I knew a bit more about shopping for fruit, and I could see that there was much, much more than five euro's worth of stuff in the bag.

Ruby folded the top of the bag and held it towards me.

'That's too much,' I said.

'Just take it,' she said almost roughly.

I could see that she was embarrassed, so I took the bag.

Ruby turned around and locked the shed door.

'Bye, Eva,' she said quietly, and then she was gone.

'Bye, and thanks,' I said to the empty space where she had been standing.

Just then, the man from the deli stall next to us came over, holding a small tub of olives towards me.

'For you,' he said.

'But what ...?' I began.

He started to laugh.

'I've been working here for seventeen years, and I've never once seen anyone get the better of Mamie. You've made my day, you really have.'

I took the olives.

'Thank you. My mum loves olives.'

The man patted me on the shoulder and left, and I smiled all the way home.

☆ ♥ ♡

'You were gone a long time,' said Mum when I got home.

'I walked slowly,' I said, as I handed her the bag of fruit.

Mum took it and peered inside.

'Wow,' she said. 'You did well. The market must be even cheaper than I thought.'

'Er, I had to haggle a bit,' I said. 'Oh, and I got something else.'

I reached into my handbag and pulled out the tub of olives.

Mum didn't say anything. She opened the tub, took out an olive and bit into it. A slow smile spread across her face.

'I was afraid I'd never again eat an olive,' she sighed.

I thought with regret of how often I'd seen our housekeeper, Teresita, throwing out olives that had been going mouldy in the fridge, after Mum had bought more than we could manage to eat.

Mum ate one more olive, and then resealed the tub and put it into the fridge, like it was the most precious thing she'd ever owned.

Then she came over and patted my head.

'That's my clever girl,' she said. 'I'll have to send you to the market again next weekend.'

'Great,' I said, trying to sound sarcastic.

But the weird thing is, I found that I was totally looking forward to it.

Chapter Sixteen

XoXo

The next week went by faster than I could have thought possible.

Dad still hadn't found a job, and he spent his days manically running around the house fixing stuff.

'I think you're fixing things that aren't even broken,' said Mum one day.

'I think he's breaking stuff just so he can fix it again,' I said.

Dad laughed, and Mum gave a big sigh. 'Well, I suppose it's good to keep yourself busy.'

I thought that she was talking to him like he was a child, but he didn't seem to mind. He put down his hammer and went over and gave her a hug and a kiss.

'Stop being gross,' I moaned. 'And anyway you two are very cheerful for poor people.'

They just laughed.

'And you're very cheeky for a small person,' said Dad.

Then the three of us laughed, and for a few minutes we were all happy.

✯ ♥ ♡

On Friday, Mr Gowing came in to the class looking a bit flustered.

'Today we're having a very important visitor,' he said.

He went on to tell us how the school had applied for a big grant to buy new computers, and that the chairperson of the grant committee was coming to tour the school.

'Will she ask us questions, Sir?' asked Chloe.

'Possibly. And if she does, only put up your hand if you're *absolutely* certain of the answer.'

As he said that, he stared at Shannon who always puts up her hand, even when she hasn't the faintest notion of the answer.

'Anyway,' said Mr Gowing. 'This is an important day for the school, so I need everyone to be on their very best behaviour – especially you, Petronella. See if you can behave yourself just this once!'

Ella gave a big sigh, and the rest of us laughed.

In the middle of maths class the classroom door opened and the principal, Mrs Parker came in with the visitor, Mrs Connery.

Mrs Connery was a huge woman. She was wearing a very ugly, very tight flowery dress, and so much jewellery that she rattled every time she moved. She was like a walking wind-chime. She spoke in a sharp, loud posh voice.

'I *loooove* mathematics,' she said. 'Can I ask the children a question?'

Mr Gowing nodded.

Mrs Connery thought for a minute and then smiled, showing a huge mouthful of horse-like teeth.

'If I had three cakes and my friend gave me four more, what would I have?'

Most of the class looked at each other, puzzled. That seemed like much too easy a problem for our class. Maybe it was a trick question.

Suddenly Shannon's hand shot up. Mr Gowing didn't look too worried. He must have thought that even Shannon couldn't get this one wrong.

'Well, little girl,' said Mrs Connery, treating Shannon to a close-up of her horrible teeth. 'If I have three cakes, and get four more, what would I have?'

Shannon beamed at her.

'You'd have a huge, big, fat belly,' she said.

We all fell around the place laughing, while Shannon looked hurt.

'What?' she said.

Mrs Connery's face went very pink and angry

for a minute, and then she recovered.

'Oh, Mr Gowing,' she gushed. 'What wonderful work you are doing with these daaaahling little children.'

'Maybe it's time to move on to the next class,' said Mrs Parker, heading for the door.

Just then Ella nudged me and pointed at Joshua. He was tearing a large strip from the page of his maths book. He crumpled it up, put it into his mouth and chewed for a second. Then he took it out, and balanced it on his thumb.

'He wouldn't dare,' breathed Ella.

'He—'

Before I could finish, Joshua lined up his middle finger and took aim. The gross squishy ball sailed through the air. It seemed to hover for a long moment, before descending and ending up right down inside the front of . . . Mrs Connery's dress.

Mrs Connery screeched like she'd been shot.

Mrs Parker looked like she was going to explode with anger.

Mr Gowing put his head in his hands and groaned.

It was the funniest thing I had ever, ever seen.

☆ ♥ ♡

That night I phoned Victoria to tell her the story.

'So I take it your school won't be getting the computer grant?' she said, as soon as she'd stopped laughing.

'That's the best part,' I said. 'Amy heard Mrs Connery telling Mrs Parker that it was clear we needed all the help we could get. The new computers arrive next week.'

'So your new school isn't all bad?' she said.

'No,' I admitted. 'And I forgot to tell you, I came top of the class in Geography yesterday.'

'But you've always been rubbish at Geography.'

I smiled to myself.

'Not any more. Mr Gowing manages to make

it so interesting, it seems easy now.'

Victoria sighed.

'Sometimes my school seems very boring compared to yours,' she said.

'Be careful what you wish for,' I warned her.

'Anyway,' she said. 'I'd better go. Mum's shouting at me to do my piano practice. See you tomorrow at Po—'

She stopped.

'Sorry, Eva,' I forgot,' she said.

'That's OK,' I said, even though it totally wasn't.

You see, pony club was paid for six months in advance, and the time I'd paid for had run out a few weeks earlier. There was no way I could afford to go any more.

'It's not the same without you,' she said.

I could feel tears of self-pity gathering in my eyes, but I shook them angrily away.

'Give Jewel a hug for me,' I said, and then I hung up, not trusting myself to say any more.

Chapter Seventeen

Next morning, Mum handed me five euro. 'Here, Eva,' she said. 'Go and do your magic in the market again.'

I put the money into my pocket, and grabbed my hoodie.

'I might be a while,' I said. 'I might meet up with some of my friends.'

'No problem,' said Mum. 'Just be home in time for lunch.'

Once again, there was a big crowd around Ruby's stall.

Who ever would have thought that potatoes and carrots and onions would be so popular?

Without saying anything, I slipped behind the

stall, and took my place beside Ruby. She glanced at me but didn't say anything. She didn't smile either, but her face didn't look quite as closed and suspicious as usual. I decided to take that as a good sign.

We quickly fell in to a routine. I weighed and packed the fruit and vegetables, while Ruby took the money and gave the change.

'Uh-oh,' said Ruby after a while.

I looked up to see Mamie advancing towards us.

'She doesn't look happy,' I said, suddenly feeling guilty about the bad apple I'd given her the week before.

'Don't worry about it,' said Ruby. 'She never looks happy,'

Mamie pointed a bony finger in my face.

'You gave me a bad apple last week,' she said.

I smiled my best innocent smile.

'I wasn't here last week. It must have been my identical twin sister. She's very naughty. How about I make it up to you by giving you a special deal on bananas?'

She narrowed her eyes.

'How special?'

'Seven for a euro, ' I said, looking her straight in the eye. 'This is a special deal, just for you. I swear to you, no one else has got bananas at this price today.'

I wasn't telling a lie. It *was* a deal specially for Mamie. You see, Ruby's uncle had ordered extra bananas by mistake. We had to get rid of them before they went bad, so all that morning we'd been selling nine for a euro.

Mamie had a cunning look on her face.

'How about eight for a euro?' she said in a pathetic, whiny voice.

I gave a big theatrical sigh.

'You drive a very hard bargain,' I said.

Mamie smiled, showing a mouthful of rotten brown teeth.

'I know,' she said happily, as she paid for her bananas and went on her way.

The man from the stall next door came over.

'You're better than a pantomime,' he said. 'This is for you!'

He handed me a small paper-wrapped bundle. I half opened it to see a small chunk of crumbly cheese with blue lines running through it. The strong smell attacked my nostrils at once.

'Thank you,' I said, turning and putting it safely into my handbag.

My handbag would smell of stinky socks for weeks, but I knew it would be worth it to see Dad's face when I gave him a present of his favourite cheese.

Hanging around the market was turning out to have lots of unexpected advantages.

✯ ❤ ♡

The morning passed very quickly, and before I knew it, Ruby and I were once again packing up the stall for the day.

'Do you want some fruit?' asked Ruby.

'Oh, yes, please,' I said fishing in my pocket for the five euro, and handing it to her.

She waved the money away. 'You've helped me,' she said. 'I can't take your money.'

'But—' I began.

'No,' she said, almost fiercely. 'I can't take your money. I should be paying you for all the work you've done this morning, but I can't afford to. So at least let me give you some stuff.'

I put my hand on her arm. 'It's OK, Ruby,' I said. 'I don't mind helping, and I don't have anything else to do on Saturday mornings.'

Now that I can't afford to go to pony club any more.

Ruby pulled her arm away.

'It's easy for you,' she said. 'You don't know what it's like to be poor.'

Ha.

I hadn't a whole lot of experience in the past,

but I was learning quickly.

Then I looked closer at Ruby. Her clothes were cheap and old-fashioned. I wouldn't be buying new clothes any time soon, but my old ones were a whole lot nicer than anything I'd ever seen Ruby wear.

By now Ruby had filled a huge bag with fruit and vegetables. I knew this wasn't a time for arguing, so I put my money back into my pocket, and took the bag from her.

'So can I help you again next Saturday?' I asked.

She looked up, and her hair fell back from her face, giving me a rare look at her huge brown eyes.

'If you want to.'

I nodded.

'I do want to.'

'Thanks,' she said, and as she turned away, I thought I could see the tiniest hint of a smile on her face.

☆ ♥ ♡

I thought I was getting used to my new life, but that all changed when I went to visit Victoria at her place the next day.

She led me through the huge hallway, where I walked extra slowly so I could enjoy the beautiful smell from the big bowl of lilies on the hall table.

The carpet on the stairs was so thick, that I could feel my feet sinking in to it. If Victoria hadn't been right in front of me, I think I'd have bent down and rubbed my hands all over its rich softness.

I'd always liked Victoria's bedroom, but now it seemed even nicer than before. One wall was painted in swirls of bright pink and purple, and her bed was covered with a huge heap of matching fluffy cushions. Her wardrobes were painted white, with cute heart-shaped handles. I didn't need to look inside to know that they were full of all the clothes she'd bought on her recent trip to

London with her parents.

I wanted to live like this.

I deserved to live like this.

And I was still being nice.

I was helping loads of people.

I was helping Ruby.

So why weren't Madam Margarita's words coming true?

Why wasn't I back where I belonged?

Why wasn't I back in my real life?

I sat on Victoria's bright pink inflatable chair, and she threw herself on to the fluffy purple rug.

'How was pony club?' I asked.

'OK,' she said cautiously, like owning up to enjoying it would have been a crime.

'It's OK,' I said. 'Just because I can't go, that doesn't mean you can't have fun.'

She smiled at me gratefully. 'So what did you do yesterday?' she asked.

'I went to the market and spent the morning

helping a girl from my class to sell fruit and vegetables,' I said.

'Yeah right,' she said laughing. 'But really, what did you do?'

I didn't answer. I couldn't blame Victoria for not believing me about the market. After all, if someone had told me a few months earlier how my life would have changed, I wouldn't have believed them either.

Only trouble was – it was all too true.

But some things are much too complicated to explain.

So I just shrugged and said, 'Not much really.'

Chapter Eighteen

I wouldn't say I was getting to like my new school, but after a while I didn't hate it quite as much.

Dawn was always really kind to me. She gave me an extra-big smile whenever she saw me.

I don't know if she ever figured out how I'd been involved in the way her life changed.

Maybe she just remembered seeing me that day, and thinking about it made her feel happy.

I wouldn't ever want to spend a whole lot of time with Mr Gowing (after all, he was a teacher), but I have to admit that he was turning out to be quite nice. Soon I decided that, as teachers go, he was probably as good as it gets.

He seemed to like me too. (Maybe that was because every time there was a horrible job to be done, I was the first to volunteer. And whenever anyone in the class was struggling with their work, I nearly tripped over myself in my rush to be the one to help.)

Most days I sat with Ella, Chloe and Amy. At first I felt guilty when I saw Ruby on her own at the other side of the classroom. But then I noticed that any time I caught her eye, she gave me a fierce look, which I took to mean that she wanted me to stay away. In the end I decided that sometimes she was quite happy to be on her own, and I even though I couldn't really understand it, I began to admire her independence.

✩ ♥ ♡

The next Saturday, I went to the market even earlier than usual. Ruby looked surprised, but she didn't say anything. As the day went on, she never got exactly talkative, but we did chat a bit.

It turned out that she was quite funny – in her own very, very quiet way.

After a few hours, I'd just finished serving a nice old man, when I looked up and saw something that shook me for a second. It was Emily, one of my old friends from The Abbey. She was with a girl I didn't know.

'Hey, Emily,' I said without thinking – without remembering that Emily hadn't contacted me for months.

Emily turned. She looked at me for a long time.

'Oh, hi,' she said in the end.

'So how's it—?' I began, but she was already walking away.

'Who was that?' asked the girl with Emily.

'Oh, no one. Just someone I sort of knew a very long time ago.'

I felt a sudden flare of anger.

She said I was no one.

How dare she?

I sat next to her for two whole years.

I invited her to my birthday party.

She ate three slices of my birthday cake.

Suddenly I realised that the banana I was holding was squashed to a pulp in my clenched fist.

Then I felt a gentle hand on my arm. Ruby took the squashed banana from my hand and put it in the bucket of damaged stuff that she saves as pig food.

'Know what?' she said quietly. 'That girl should cop on to herself and make a bit more effort with her appearance.'

I looked at Emily who had stopped at a stall nearby.

'But she…' I began before I noticed the wicked smirk on Ruby's face.

'You're joking,' I said and Ruby nodded.

I looked at Emily in her turquoise high heels, which matched her turquoise handbag, which matched her turquoise eyeshadow, which matched her turquoise nail varnish, which matched her turquoise belt, which matched her ... well you get the idea. Emily was dressed for the Teen Choice Awards, not a Saturday morning in the market. She looked totally ridiculous – and that made me very, very happy.

I grinned at Ruby, but she had already turned away to tidy the vegetables.

✯ ♥ ♡

When the market was over, I helped Ruby to close up the stall.

Once again, she gave me a huge bag of fruit and vegetables.

Once again she refused the five euro that I offered her.

But this time she didn't vanish as soon as the bag of food was safely in my arms. We stood together outside the locked-up shed. Ruby looked embarrassed, and that made me feel embarrassed too.

I'd never before spent so much time in the company of someone so strange – or someone I knew so little about.

'I'd better go home,' I said in the end.

'Wait,' she said.

I waited, but for a long time, nothing happened, except that Ruby's cheeks turned from pale pink to deeper pink and then to a strong dark red that matched her name perfectly. Then she was muttering, 'I got you something.'

She put her hand into her pocket and then removed it, holding her closed fist towards me.

I wondered what she wanted to give me. The thing I wanted right then was a big pile of fifty euro notes, or the winning ticket for that night's lottery, and there wasn't much chance Ruby was going to give me either of those.

This girl was so weird I half expected her to say that she was giving me her pet slug.

'I've noticed that you like purple,' she said.

Not a slug, so.

Maybe it was a very pretty grape or a squashed-up flower.

I love getting presents, but I couldn't bring myself to look forward to this one.

I rearranged the bag of fruit and vegetables so that it was propped up on my hip, held steady with my left hand. Then, very slowly and cautiously, I stretched out the open palm of my right hand.

Very slowly and cautiously, Ruby opened her fist, and something dropped from her hand into mine.

Then we stood there, like an evil fairy had turned us into stone.

'Wow,' I gasped when I'd got tired of standing there, looking like an idiot made of stone.

I'm used to beautiful things, but I think this might have been the most beautiful thing I had ever seen. I was a bracelet made of tiny purple and mauve beads. As I moved my hand, the bracelet shimmered in the light, almost like it was half alive.

'Wow,' I said again, just before I realised that I couldn't take presents from Ruby. How could I take anything from a girl who had so little?

'But I can't ……' I began.

Ruby jumped back like I had punched her.

'It's OK. I didn't buy it,' she said.

For one second a horrible thought floated into my mind.

'I didn't steal it either, if that's what you're thinking,' she said.

I shook my head. 'I'd never think that of you,' I said, telling a total lie.

I looked at the bracelet again, and slipped it on to my wrist.

It felt cool and silky against my skin.

It matched my purple top perfectly.

'My mum made it,' said Ruby. 'I told her I wanted to give you something for helping me, so she made you this. I hope you like it.'

I stepped forwards ready to hug her, then decided against it. Ruby *so* wasn't a huggy kind of girl.

'I don't like it,' I said.

Ruby's face fell, and I rushed to finish what I had started to say.

'I *love* it. I absolutely love it.'

Then, for the first time ever, I saw Ruby give a proper smile, and it was almost like she had given me another present.

As we walked out from the market together, I saw Ella coming along the street with Chloe and Amy. I felt a sudden flush of embarrassment. The more I got to know Ruby, the more I liked her, but the other girls probably still thought of her as the class loser. I wondered for a second if I could duck back into the market, but before I could move, the girls were in front of us. Beside me, I could feel Ruby becoming tense and alert – like she was ready to be offended.

But I needn't have worried.

'Hey, Eva. Hey Ruby,' said Ella, like seeing us together was the most normal thing in the world. 'We're going for hot chocolate. Do you want to come?'

'No,' said Ruby.

'We'd love to,' I said at the same time, and half-dragging Ruby behind me, I followed the girls into the coffee shop.

'Let me buy you a hot chocolate,' I said to Ruby, brandishing my five euro note.

She shook her head fiercely. 'I can pay for myself,' she muttered, and I realised that I had insulted her proud spirit.

'Whatever,' I said, half-relieved that I'd be bringing most of the money back home to Mum and Dad.

Soon the five of us were seated around a big table, stirring marshmallows into our hot chocolate and talking about stuff. Ruby didn't exactly look relaxed, but she didn't look like she wanted to run away and hide either.

'Hey, Eva, cool bracelet,' said Amy as I reached for extra sugar.

'Ruby's mum made it,' I said.

'No way,' said Chloe.

I nodded. 'It's true.'

'Wow,' said Ella. 'She must be a genius.'

I turned to Ruby. Her face was red, but I could see that she was pleased.

It turned out to be a lovely day.

Chapter Nineteen

On Sunday, Victoria came to spend the day at my place.

'Wow,' she said when she came inside. 'Did you get a new kitchen put in?'

Dad smiled.

'No,' he said, puffing up with pride. 'That's the old kitchen. A friend gave me a few cans of paint he didn't need, and I used it to paint the units. Nice aren't they?'

'Totally,' said Victoria.

I wondered if she was being sincere. I couldn't help comparing Dad's handiwork with the very flashy maple and steel kitchen that Victoria's parents had had fitted in their house a few months earlier.

'I'm doing the bathroom next,' said Dad. 'First I'm going to re-grout the tiles, and then I'm going to sand the floorboards, and then—'

'Dad,' I wailed. 'Victoria isn't here for a DIY lesson.'

'Oh,' said Dad, disappointed.

I grabbed Victoria's arm and pulled her towards the hall.

'Come on,' I said. 'Before he gets started again.'

Victoria laughed, and followed me.

'Your dad's changed,' she said as we went upstairs.'

'Tell me about it!' I said.

'Don't knock it. Some changes are good you know. And your mum – she seems kind of different these days too.'

I smiled.

'Yes she is, isn't she? She always used to go out to lunch and coffee mornings and stuff – but she never had any real friends. Now that's all changed though. She's forever having the neighbours in for cups of tea. They're always teaching her these weird recycled craft things, and talking about allotments and stuff. Sometimes I can't concentrate on my homework, they're laughing so much.'

'That's good isn't it?'

I shrugged.

'I suppose so,' I conceded.

✡ ❤ ♡

'So, any real news?' said Victoria when we were settled in my room.

Before I could answer, she noticed my new bracelet on my wrist. She leaned over and touched it, running her fingers along the tiny, shimmering beads.

'That is so, so beautiful,' she said. 'Where did you get it?'

'You mean "where did a poor girl like me get

such a beautiful bracelet"?' I snapped.

Victoria shook her head.

'Stop being so defensive, Eva. I mean it's a beautiful bracelet, and I've never seen it before and I'm wondering where you got it.'

'Sorry,' I said.

She smiled.

'And?'

I hesitated.

I *so* didn't want to tell Victoria about Ruby and the market.

I didn't know how to say it without making myself sound like a loser.

But Victoria was my best friend in the whole world, and how could I be proper friends with someone I kept telling lies to?

So I took a deep breath, and told Victoria all about Ruby, and how I'd started to help her in the market on Saturdays.

Victoria listened to my story with a puzzled

expression on her face.

'That's really nice of you, and everything, but … er … why?' she said in the end.

'Why what?'

Victoria sighed.

'This is what I'm hearing. There's this girl, that you don't seem to like very much, and she doesn't seem to like you – or anyone else – that much.'

'I wouldn't exactly say that I don't like her,' I corrected Victoria. 'It's just that she's different to anyone I've ever known before.'

'Whatever. She's in your class, but she doesn't talk to you at school, and you don't talk to her?'

'Well…yes.'

'And yet you spend all of your Saturday mornings helping her to sell cabbages in the market.'

I giggled.

'Pay attention. It's not just cabbages. We sell carrots, broccoli, apples, oranges. We have a very wide range of produce!'

Victoria giggled too.

'Well you know what I'm trying to say. I mean, you've always been a nice girl and everything, but you're not a saint. So why are you doing this?'

I hesitated again.

It was one thing telling Victoria about Ruby.

Did I really want to tell her about Madam Margarita as well?

But Victoria was smiling at me, and I knew that if anyone in the whole world was going to understand this crazy story, it had to be Victoria. So I took another deep breath, and told her all about what Madam Margarita had said.

When I had finished, Victoria was silent for a long time.

I figured that silence was better than laughter, but it still wasn't exactly the reaction I had hoped for.

'Well?' I said when I couldn't take any more.

'So this fortune-teller woman, that I was

stupid enough to let you talk to, tells you to do loads of good deeds, and then you'll get what you want?'

I nodded.

'And you believe her?' she asked.

'Wouldn't you?'

She shook her head.

'Sorry, Eva, but I don't think I would.'

Why was I surprised?

'It's easy for you,' I said. 'You already have everything you want. You don't know what it's like to want something as badly as I do.'

'So what exactly is it that you want?'

'I'm not greedy,' I answered. 'I only want one thing.'

'And that is?'

'I want my old life back.'

Victoria giggled.

'It might only be one thing, but it's a very big one thing, don't you think?'

I sighed.

'I know. But it's all I want. I want my old house, my old life – the whole lot. I might not have appreciated it properly at the time, but I'd sure appreciate it now.'

'But in your old life, you didn't know Ella, and now she's a really good friend.'

'That's true,' I conceded. 'So I'll change my wish. I wish I had my old life back, just with Ella in it. How does that sound?'

'Complicated.'

She was right, but I didn't acknowledge that.

I sighed, again.

'My biggest wish is that one day I'll wake up and realise that these last few months have been a very long, very bad dream.'

Victoria shook her head.

'Sorry to disappoint you, Eva, but this isn't a dream.'

'I know,' I said quickly. 'And that's why I have

to believe in Madam Margarita.'

Even as I said the last words, I knew they weren't true. I'd never really, really truly believed in her. I had just wanted to believe in her. And now, after weeks of doing as she suggested, nothing had changed.

Madam Margarita had to be a fraud.

Why hadn't I been able to see it before?

I felt a sick feeling in my stomach as the last strands of hope vanished, like the string of a runaway balloon slipping through my fingers. My dream was disappearing before my eyes.

I sighed again.

'You're right. It's not going to work. I was crazy to ever think that it would.'

Victoria came over and hugged me. I could smell the expensive fabric conditioner on her hoodie. It was the kind my mum used to use – back when we could still afford it.

'I'm so sorry, Eva,' said Victoria, when I finally,

reluctantly let her go.

I tried to smile. 'Maybe the first twenty years of being poor are the hardest. It'll probably be OK after that.'

She smiled. 'I'm sure things aren't that bad. And, look on the bright side, now that you know Madam Margarita was talking rubbish, you can forget all about her advice. You can forget about helping people. You can forget all about working in the market.'

I started to smile, but then changed my mind.

'No, Victoria,' I said. 'I can't stop working in the market.'

Victoria shook her head in frustration.

'I don't get you sometimes, Eva. I really don't.'

I wrinkled up my face as I tried to explain.

'You see, at first, I only helped Ruby because of what Madam Margarita said. I was helping her because I stupidly believed that it would somehow end up helping me. But now things are different. I know Ruby is a bit weird – well actually she's very weird – but she's nice too, and she needs help, and if I don't help her, who else will?'

Victoria hugged me again.

'You're the kindest girl I've ever met,' she said, and I was embarrassed, but very, very pleased.

Chapter Twenty

Soon it was Saturday again, and I took my place beside Ruby at the fruit and vegetable stall. I was starting to get to know the customers now, and some of them greeted me like I was one of their oldest friends. Even Mamie sort of smiled at me sometimes. I think she was glad that at last someone was tough enough to stand up to her.

The morning went really quickly, and soon I found myself standing outside the locked-up shed, holding my usual bag of food.

Once again, Ruby looked embarrassed.

'Want to come to my place for a while?' she asked.

I was so surprised I didn't know what to say. I looked carefully at her, and got the horrible feeling that she was really, really hoping that I was going to say no.

'Er … I'm not sure,' I said, stalling for time. 'My mum and dad will be expecting me home.'

'Can't you text them and tell them you're going to be a bit late?' now she sounded desperate.

What was going on?

Did this girl want me to go to her place or not?

And if she didn't, why was she asking me in the first place?

'My mum said I should ask you,' said Ruby in the end. 'I told her how you've been helping me on the stall, and she said that the least we could do is invite you over for some lunch.'

Suddenly I felt even more sorry for Ruby than usual. I had a funny feeling that she didn't often ask friends to her place.

I had a funny feeling that she didn't have any friends.

Did she think I was her friend?

And what would her mother say to her if she arrived home without me?

So I smiled at her.

'Sure,' I said. 'I'd love to come over to your place for a while.' Then I sent a quick text to my mum, and followed Ruby down the street.

Neither of us said much as we walked along. I didn't mind. I was getting used to Ruby's long silences – and sometimes it's kind of relaxing not to have to talk.

'Nearly there,' said Ruby at last, as we turned a corner.

'Hey, I know this road,' I said. 'I've been here before. Madam Margarita lives here, doesn't she?'

Ruby glared at me.

'What do you know about Madam Margarita?'

Her fierce look made me think that this wasn't a time for telling the truth.

'Oh, I just heard someone talking about her once,' I said.

Ruby still looked fierce, but she didn't ask any more questions.

'Here we are,' she said a moment later. 'Home sweet home.'

I gulped.

The sign was gone, but that didn't matter. I'd recognise the front door with its flaky blue paint anywhere.

There were hundreds of streets, and thousands and thousands of houses in our town.

So, of all the houses in all the streets, why was Ruby leading me towards Madam Margarita's one?

I thought about running away, but before I could move, Ruby had flung open the front door.

'Mum, I'm home,' she called. 'And I've brought my friend, Eva.'

I gulped again.

What on earth had I left myself in for?

✩ ♥ ♡

In a daze, I followed Ruby in the front door and through the hallway. Nothing had changed since my last visit. Everything still looked dark and dull and dreary, making me wonder if maybe my new home wasn't as bad as I thought.

I followed Ruby in to the kitchen. I stood there with my mouth open and watched as Madam Margarita's mouth opened equally wide.

'It's the Princess,' said Madam Margarita. 'Ruby, you've brought the Princess.'

'It's Madam Margarita,' I said. 'Ruby, you've brought me to see Madam Margarita.'

Ruby looked at us like we were both totally crazy.

'I didn't know you were a princess,' she

snapped at me. 'You've managed not to mention that before. And that's certainly not Madam Margarita. That's my mum and her name is Maggie.' Ruby stopped speaking and for a second I felt that I could hear the cogs in her brain revolving as she tried to figure out what was going on.

'I get it,' she said in the end. 'Eva is the one.'

'What one?' I asked.

'The one who came to see Madam Margarita. The only customer Madam Margarita, or should I say Maggie, ever had.'

'So you're not a real fortune-teller?' I said.

Maggie shook her head. 'Well, no, not exactly.'

Now I felt really angry. I was cross with Maggie, but mostly I was cross with myself for believing all the rubbish she had told me.

'But that's not fair,' I said. 'You're an imposter. You took ten euro from me under false pretences. There are laws against that kind of thing. I should go straight to the police and report you.'

'I'm ……' began Maggie but I interrupted her. I wasn't angry anymore – I just felt sad and stupid.

'You tricked me,' I said. 'You made me believe what you said was true, and that so isn't fair.'

Maggie spoke softly.

'I didn't mean any harm. And I did read two books about fortune-telling. And I was going to read another few, but they didn't have any more in the library.'

Was this woman for real?

Did she expect me to be impressed because she'd read a few books on fortune-telling?

I read a book about space exploration once – did that mean I could sign up for the next rocket to the moon?

Ruby didn't look very happy either.

'What did you tell Eva, Mum?' she asked in a cold voice. 'Did you tell her that there was going to be a tall handsome stranger in her life? I suppose you'd have been half right. Mr Gowing is tall, and he certainly is strange. He's not handsome though. But still, two out of three's not bad – for someone who has read two whole books in the library!'

Now I felt angry again.

Was Ruby mocking me?

How dare she?

How would she feel if I told her what Maggie had really told me?

How would she feel if she knew that I only helped her because of what her mother had said?

How would she feel if ......?

I looked at Ruby, standing against the counter, looking like she'd happily kill her mother or me, or both of us.

I looked at Maggie next to her, looking nervous and guilty.

They were both staring at me with identical,

huge brown eyes.

How had I managed not to notice the resemblance before?

Suddenly I couldn't concentrate any more – I was too busy laughing.

This whole thing was really very funny.

Madam Margarita asked me to do something, and doing it led me right back to her doorstep.

How weird was that?

After a second, Maggie and Ruby started to laugh too. The three of us laughed until there were tears streaming from our eyes. I stopped when the pain in my side became too much. I wiped my eyes and looked at the others. Ruby was leaning on Maggie's wheelchair, and Maggie had her arm around her daughter's waist. Maggie looked young and pretty, and for the first time since I'd met her, Ruby looked like a normal girl, having fun.

At last Maggie stopped laughing too.

'Thanks for coming, Eva,' she said. 'I've made some chicken wraps. Would you like one?'

I giggled.

'You're the fortune-teller. Why don't you tell me?' I said, and then we all laughed some more, before sitting down for our lunch.

☆ ♥ ♡

After we had eaten, I helped Ruby to clear the table, and then I said that I'd better go.

'It's starting to rain,' said Maggie as we got to the door. 'Ruby, why don't you run upstairs and get Eva a jacket to wear home?'

Ruby ran upstairs, and Maggie wheeled herself closer to me.

'Thank you so much for helping Ruby out these last few weeks. It means a lot to her, and to me.'

'That's OK,' I said, feeling embarrassed.

'Ruby isn't very good at making friends,' she continued.

Ha! That was an understatement. Ruby was a total disaster at making friends.

Before either of us could say any more, Ruby was back, holding the ugliest jacket I'd ever seen.

'Oh look,' I said brightly. 'The rain has stopped. Bye now, and thanks for everything.'

Then I skipped out the door, before anyone could point out that there were torrents of water pouring from the sky.

Chapter Twenty-One

That night, I told Mum and Dad about Maggie and Ruby. I left out the Madam Margarita part, as I figured the story was complicated enough without dragging that into the middle of it.

'So that's what happened,' I said, as I came to the end of the story. 'One day, everything was fine – well sort of fine anyway. Maggie was running the stall, and Ruby got to be a normal kid. Then, when Maggie fell off her bike and hurt her back, everything changed in an instant.'

'And it's just the two of them in the family?' asked Dad.

I shook my head.

'No. Ruby has a big sister called Jenny. She's training to be a hairdresser. She works really long hours, but gets paid hardly anything. So the whole family has to survive on what they can earn at the market.'

'That's a really sad story,' said Mum.

I nodded.

'Sad and weird. One day, months and months ago, Maggie closed her bedroom door and came downstairs, and she's never been able to go back up since then. She has to sleep in the living room, and there's not even any room there for her clothes. Ruby has to spend her time going up and down the stairs getting stuff for her.'

Mum patted my arm.

'Well, all I can say is that Dad and I are very proud of you for the way you've been helping Ruby.'

'Thanks,' I said. 'But I wish I could do more to help. Helping out in the market for a few hours doesn't seem like enough. Why can't I do more?'

No one answered.

Mum smiled sympathetically, but Dad just sat there saying nothing. That started to make me worried. Dad isn't good at silence – he's more the doing type of man.

I wondered what kind of weird scheme was running through his brain.

✩ ♥ ♡

Dad called me early the next morning.

'Wake up, Eva,' he said. 'We need to talk.'

I rubbed my eyes, checked the time on my phone and closed my eyes again.

'Go away, Dad,' I said. 'It's still the middle of the night.'

'But this is important, Eva,' he said.

'Nothing is important enough to wake a girl up at eight o'clock on a Sunday.'

He didn't move.

My dad is totally stubborn, and I knew he

wasn't going to give in any time soon.

I gave a big sigh, and sat up in bed.

Once upon a time I'd have been expecting a big present or a nice surprise at a time like this. Now, though, I knew for sure that Dad wasn't going to produce a piece of perfect jewellery from his jacket pocket.

'This had better be worth it,' I muttered.

Dad sat on the edge of my bed.

'What are the stairs in your friend Ruby's house like?'

Great. My dad wasn't just poor and unemployed – now he was crazy too.

I pretended to think.

'Oh yes,' I said in the end. 'The stairs in Ruby's house start on the ground floor, they go all the way up to the next floor, and they've got lots of steps in between.'

'Very funny,' said Dad. 'What I mean is, are they straight or curved?'

I stopped trying to decide if my dad had gone crazy, and instead tried to picture Ruby running up the stairs the day before.

'Straight,' I said, after a second.

'*Yesss*!' said Dad like he'd just won the lottery. 'Now get dressed. We've got a lot to do.'

I decided that I'd indulged him enough. I folded my arms.

'Sorry, Dad. I don't do dressed this early on Sundays.'

Dad sighed.

'Just listen, Eva. I hardly slept last night, because I couldn't stop thinking about your friends. And at some stage in the early hours of the morning, I remembered something that happened a few months ago. A man I used to work with told me about his brother who had bought a house.'

'Very exciting,' I said. 'I'm glad you woke me up to tell me that. I hope your friend's brother is very happy in his new home. Now, can I go back to sleep?'

Dad ignored me. 'And his brother had to do loads of jobs in the house before he could move in. And one of the jobs he had to do was to take out the stair-lift belonging to the man who owned the house before him.'

At last this was starting to make sense.

'And?'

'And I phoned my friend this morning and as soon as he got over being cross with me for waking him so early, he told me that the stair-lift was still in his brother's shed, and that we could have it if we wanted.'

'But—'

'And also in the shed is the old man's wheelchair. It's a bit of a wreck, but it would do fine for Maggie to keep upstairs so that she could go from room to room when she's up there.'

I was already out of bed.

'Why are you still here, Dad? Get out. I want to get dressed.'

Dad laughed.

'We leave in five minutes.'

✯ ❤ ♡

At first Maggie thought we were messing.

I think part of her still thought we were messing when Dad and I started to unload his tools from the back of Mum's car.

She still didn't look convinced when another friend of Dad's drew up in his van and started to unload the parts of what was very obviously a stair-lift.

Many, many hours later, when the lift was carrying Maggie up her own stairs for the first time in months, I think she had figured out that this wasn't just some sick practical joke.

But I couldn't say for sure what she was feeling.

The tears streaming down her face were the only clue.

Chapter Twenty-Two

At school on Monday, I tried not to look too surprised when Ruby came over to me. Up to this, she had always acted like I became invisible the second I walked through the school gates.

Did she want to be friends at last?

And how did I feel about that?

Before I could make up my mind, she was next to me, and whispering in my ear.

'I haven't seen my mum this happy for a very long time. Thank you,' she said.

'That's OK,' I said. 'Dad likes to fix stuff, and he likes helping people.'

'So he's a lot like you,' said Ruby, making me feel really, really bad.

I looked around the room, wondering how quickly I could escape to Ella and my other friends.

'My mum would love to do something to thank you, but she doesn't know what,' said Ruby then.

'There's no need ...' I started to say, before a thought that had been circling around my mind for a while, suddenly fought its way to the surface.

'You remember that bracelet your mum made me?'

Ruby nodded.

'Would you like her to make you another one? I know she'd be happy to. What colour would you like this time?'

I hesitated.

'Well, I don't want to sound greedy, but could

she make me more than one?'

'You mean like two?'

'I was thinking more like ten.'

Ruby didn't answer, so I tried to explain. 'You know, I could wear a few at a time, and if your mum could do a few different colours, that would be great too, so I could wear them with all different outfits.....and stuff.'

Clearly Ruby thought that I was being very, very greedy, but after what Dad and I had done for her mother, how could she argue?

'I suppose so,' she said doubtfully. 'But it might take her a few days.'

'That's OK,' I said. 'Tell her there's no rush.'

I bent to put my school bag on my desk, and when I looked up again, Ruby had slipped away to the far corner of the classroom.

Then Ella was beside me.

'Hi, Eva,' she said. 'I had such a fun weekend. Did you do anything exciting?'

I shook my head.

'Not a thing. Why don't you just tell me your news?'

As we went off arm in arm, I could see Ruby watching from the other side of the classroom.

And I was fairly sure that she was smiling.

☆ ❤ ♡

After lunch that day, I raced through the maths assignment that Mr Gowing had set us, and then I slipped to the corner of the classroom where Dawn was working on the computer.

'Hi, Eva,' she said, smiling the happy smile that rarely left her face these days.

'Hi, Dawn,' I said. 'Have you time to help me with something on the computer? It's to do with a project.'

Dawn narrowed her eyes.

'Is it just me, or do you seem to be always working on a different project to everyone else in this class?'

I smiled as I remembered the imaginary butterfly project. That seemed like it had happened a very long time ago.

'It's just an extra thing I'm doing,' I said. 'Now can we get started?'

Twenty minutes later, I had done exactly what I wanted on the computer, and Dawn printed it out for me.

'I suppose you want it laminated too?' she said.

I smiled sweetly. 'Yes please.'

She shook her head, pretending to be cross.

'I'm going down to the office in a few minutes, and I'll do it then, OK?'

'Thanks for your help, Dawn,' I said. 'I hope you have a really lovely time in South America.'

'How do you know about my trip to South America?'

She was totally puzzled now.

I shrugged.

'A lucky guess, I suppose.'

Dawn gave me a very funny look, and went off to the office to get my page laminated.

☆ ♥ ♡

When I got home from school that day, Mum was sitting in the kitchen having coffee with one of her new friends.

The firm where Mum used to work part-time had closed down a few weeks earlier, so these days Mum spent most of her time at home.

'Hi, Eva, this is Deirdre,' she said. 'She lives up the road. As soon as we finish our coffee, she's going to show me how to grow tomatoes.'

The thought of my mum growing tomatoes was just too weird, so I decided to change the subject.

'Where's Dad,' I said. 'I don't hear the sound of hammering so I know he can't be here.'

Mum laughed. 'He went over to Ruby's house this morning to check that the stair lift was working ok. While he was there, a neighbour of

Maggie's asked him to come over to see if his attic would be suitable for conversion. Dad thought it was suitable, and the neighbour offered him the job of doing the conversion. Dad accepted, and now he's gone to buy the stuff he needs.'

This was even weirder than Mum growing tomatoes.

My dad, who'd worked in an office for years, was now doing an attic conversion?

I rolled my eyes.

'I'm going up to do my homework,' I said. 'At least I can understand what's going on in my schoolbooks.'

Chapter Twenty-Three

The next Saturday I showed up extra-early at the market. There were no customers at the fruit stall, which suited me fine.

'I brought you your ten bracelets,' said Ruby, handing me a paper bag.

I couldn't really blame her for the way she spat out the word 'ten', like it was poison in her mouth.

'Thanks,' I said.

I opened the bag and examined the bracelets. I wouldn't have thought it possible, but some of them were even more beautiful than the first bracelet Ruby had given me. They were in various shades of blue and green and palest pink. I ran my fingers through them, enjoying the silky smoothness of them.

Then I put the bracelets down and began to pile bananas on top of each other at one side of the stall.

'What are you doing?' asked Ruby.

'Clearing a space.'

She didn't get a chance to argue, as a very fussy customer appeared asking hard questions about the varieties of apples on display.

When Ruby was free to pay attention again, I had cleared a whole section of the stall, and on it I had laid a pink silk scarf I'd 'borrowed' from my mum's wardrobe. On the scarf I had laid the bracelets, arranged in groups according to their colours. Behind the scarf, propped up on a cauliflower and a cabbage, I had placed the laminated sign that Dawn had helped me to make.

Designer Bracelets. Handmade and Exclusive.

Only Five Euro Each.

'What do you think?' I said.

Ruby looked at my display for a long time.

'You're selling the bracelets my mum made you?' she said in disgust. 'How mean can you be?'

'No, it's not like that,' I rushed to explain. 'I never wanted the bracelets for myself. I only wanted them so I could sell them. The bracelets are so beautiful, but I didn't know if you and your mum would agree to selling them on the stall. So that's why I pretended that I wanted them for myself.'

'And who gets to keep the money?'

It was a rude question, but maybe it wasn't fair to blame Ruby for that. In a family where money was so tight, there probably wasn't any room for politeness.

'You and your mum, of course.'

Ruby's face had taken on its usual blank expression.

'Why are you doing this?' she asked.

I wasn't really sure why I was doing this. It just seemed like the right thing to do.

Before I could decide on an answer, I heard a familiar voice.

'Hi, Eva.'

I looked up to see Victoria.

At first I felt a bit ashamed. There was Victoria, in a totally cool new jacket, and looking like she'd just stepped out of the hairdressers.

There was me, standing behind a pile of cabbages, with my not-totally-clean hair tied up in a scrunchie, and wearing a hoodie that I'd had for at least six months.

And then there was Ruby.

That morning, as we worked together, I'd almost managed to forget how strange Ruby was. It was only now that Victoria was there, and I tried to see Ruby through her eyes, that I remembered.

Did that make me weird too?

Or did it just make me a nicer person than I used to be?

Victoria was gushing.

'Wow, what cool bracelets! They're just like your lovely purple one. You told me you were selling parsnips and stuff. If you'd told me about these, I'd have brought all my friends.'

I grinned at her.

'Victoria, this is Ruby. Ruby, meet Victoria.'

The girls smiled at each other, and then Ruby sold a bag of potatoes while Victoria examined the bracelets more closely.

'I think I'll take this blue one for myself, and I'll take a pink one for my friend from school. It's her birthday next week. She's going to totally love it.'

'That'll be ten euro then,' I said, feeling very pleased with myself.

Ruby's mouth was wide open with surprise. I

winked at her. I wondered if, like me, she was working out how many potatoes or parsnips she'd have to sell to make that much money.

Victoria opened her purse and handed me ten euro. Then she slipped the bracelets into her coat pocket.

'Do you want to go for a hot chocolate later?' she asked.

I nodded.

'Sure. I'll be finished here at one. I'll meet you at the gateway over there.'

Victoria turned to Ruby.

'Would you like to join us?'

'Er, no thanks,' said Ruby.

'OK,' said Victoria. 'See you later, Eva.'

Then she walked off and vanished into the crowd.

✯ ❤ ♡

In less than an hour, all the bracelets were sold. I put Mum's scarf, and the laminated sign safely under the stall, and handed Ruby fifty euro.

'Wow,' was all she could say.

I think that meant that she was happy.

'How many bracelets do you think your mum could make for next week?' I asked.

Ruby shrugged.

'I don't know. Lots, I hope.'

As soon as the stall was closed up for the day, Ruby handed me my usual bag of fruit and vegetables.

'And take this,' she said.

It was five euro.

'But.....' I began.

Ruby pushed the money into my hand.

'I wish I could afford to give you more,' she said. 'But I can't. So don't offend me by saying no. OK?'

She sounded so fierce that I didn't like to argue. And besides, if I took the money, it would mean that for the first time in ages, I'd be able to buy a hot chocolate for Victoria, instead of her buying me one.

So I took the money and slipped it into my pocket. Then I waved goodbye and went to meet Victoria.

'I so love this bracelet,' Victoria said as we settled down with our drinks. 'I'm going to tell all my friends about it. I bet they'll all want to buy one too.'

'Thanks,' I said. 'That will mean a lot to Ruby and her mother. They really need the money.'

Victoria gave a sudden giggle.

'I hope you don't mind me saying this, Eva, but I think your new friend is a small bit weird.'

I giggled too.

'She's not a small bit weird. She's very weird. But it's nice weird. And you get used to it after a while. And she's really good to her mum. She does heaps of stuff for her, and she never complains. You have to admire her for that.'

'She's lucky that she met you. Look how much you and your dad have done for her family.'

I shrugged, embarrassed.

'Ruby's kind of helped me too,' I said. 'Helping her has distracted me – given me something to focus on.'

Victoria smiled.

'So it's the perfect relationship. She needs to chill though. You should persuade her to come with us for hot chocolate next Saturday.'

I nodded happily.

'Yes,' I said. 'I definitely will.'

Chapter Twenty-Four

Victoria did as she had promised and told all her friends about Maggie's bracelets; soon I was selling bracelets as fast as Maggie could make them. After a while, she designed matching necklaces, and totally cool phone charms.

One Saturday, when I showed up at the market, Ruby looked happier than I had ever seen her.

'Mum's managed to pay off all of our bills,' she said. 'So now she can afford to pay someone to help to run the stall. So from now on I'll only have to work on Saturdays, not on all the other days the market is open.'

‘That’s great news,’ I said. ‘What are you going to do with all of your free time?’

I couldn’t really imagine Ruby doing any of the kind of stuff that I liked to do. I couldn’t really imagine her doing anything except sitting at school or selling fruit and vegetables.

She didn’t hesitate.

‘I’m going to swim,’ she said.

‘Swim?’

‘Yes, you know – when you splash your arms and legs and move along in the water? Lots of people do it.’

I had to laugh. I love it when Ruby tries to be funny.

‘So you’re going to join a swimming club?’

‘No. Clubs really aren’t my thing. I just like going to the pool and swimming. I can do fifty lengths without stopping.’

I couldn’t think of many things I’d like to do less, but even talking about it made Ruby look happy, so who was I to argue?

'So, since it's my only day here, I'll be able to manage the stall on my own on Saturdays,' she said. 'Even the jewellery part.'

What was she saying?

'You don't have to help me any more if you don't want,' she said, making it clear enough for me.

Suddenly I felt very sad.

Helping Ruby in the market had become as much of my Saturday mornings as Pony Club used to be.

I looked forward to it.

I loved helping kids pick out nice bracelets and necklaces.

I loved chatting with the old people, and pretending to be hurt when they questioned the quality of the cabbages or turnips.

I loved my weekly battles with Mamie

Every week, the man from the deli stall gave

me some sort of foodie treat, and I loved bringing it home, along with a huge sack of fruit and vegetables. I loved the way Mum and Dad waited for me to come home on Saturdays. I loved the way they unpacked the bag of goodies with all the impatience of tiny kids on Christmas morning. I loved the feeling that I was giving something to my family, instead of just taking all the time.

Ruby was staring at me with her huge brown eyes.

'I've kind of got used to you being here, though,' she said. 'So if you want—'

I didn't wait for her to finish.

'I'd love to keep coming here,' I said.

Ruby looked pleased.

'I'm glad,' she said. 'But Mum and I insist on paying you properly – that's the deal.'

I didn't argue. For one thing, Ruby was giving me such a fierce look, I didn't dare to object. And besides, the thought of having some money of my own again, was something I so didn't want to say no to.

Ruby shook my hand formally.

'Agreed?'

I nodded happily, 'Agreed.'

After one of her long silences, Ruby continued. 'There's just one thing. Mum would like to talk to you. Could you come over for lunch today?'

Before I could spend any time worrying about why Ruby's mum wanted to see me, there was a little boy pulling at my sleeve.

'Miss,' he said. 'Can you help me to pick a nice bracelet for my sister? It's her birthday tomorrow.'

I turned to help him, and so another Saturday in the market began.

✩ ♥ ♡

When we got to Ruby's place, I had to blink a few

times to make sure that I was in the right place. The front door had been freshly painted, and there were pots of flowers on the doorstep.

'Wow,' I said. 'What happened here?'

'Thanks to you, we were able to pay someone to spend an afternoon doing odd-jobs, and he worked miracles.'

Ruby led me in to the front room. The bed was gone, and without it, the room looked huge – or maybe not huge, but certainly bigger than before.

The table was still there, and in the middle of it was a round goldfish bowl with a fish swimming around happily.

'Was that ...?' I began.

Ruby nodded.

'That was Mum's crystal ball. When you were here that day, she threw poor Bubbles into the washing-up basin in the kitchen.'

I giggled. It might have been cruelty to

animals, but since Bubbles didn't look too bothered, I figured there was no need for me to make a fuss about it.

I thought back to the first time I had been in the room. I remembered Maggie in the ugly turban and the cloak that looked like it was made of tin foil.

I remembered how sad and hopeless I had felt that day.

Now Maggie came in to the room. She looked younger and happier than I had ever seen her before.

'Will you go into the kitchen and set the table for lunch please, Ruby,' she said.

Ruby left the room, closing the door behind her.

Maggie reached out her hand as if to shake hands with me, but when our hands touched, she slipped a ten euro note into my fingers.

'I think I owe you this, Eva,' she said.

'But ...' I began.

'Just listen,' she said. 'On that stupid Madam Margarita sign, I wrote that I could change your life. How pathetic and arrogant was that?'

That didn't seem like a question that needed an answer, so I said nothing, and Maggie continued.

'Anyway, you noticed the sign, and came in here, and a life did get changed. But it was my life – not yours. And I am more grateful than you could ever understand. I can't ever repay you properly. Nothing could repay you properly. But at least I would like you to have the ten euro I took from you under false pretences.'

I looked at the money for a second.

I thought of all the cool things I could buy with ten euro.

Then I looked at the shabby room, and the torn carpet. If I had a hundred things to spend ten euro on, surely Maggie had thousands.

I pushed the money back into her hand.

'No,' I said firmly. 'You might have been talking rubbish that day, but I believed it for a while.'

'You did?'

I nodded, and Maggie went on.

'When I came up with the stupid fortune-telling idea, I never really expected anyone to take it seriously. I was desperate, and I thought it might be an easy way to make money. But you believed what I said?'

I nodded again.

'I'm so sorry,' she said. 'It was wrong of me to take advantage of you.'

'But I *wanted* to believe you,' I said. 'I *needed* to believe you.'

Now Maggie looked more embarrassed than ever.

'I'm so sorry, Eva,' she said. 'It was a long time ago. I can't even remember what I told you that day.'

'You said that if I helped people, my life would get better.'

She nodded slowly.

'Of course – I remember now. You see, at the time I thought you were a spoiled little princess, but how wrong I was!'

I shook my head.

'But you weren't wrong. I was totally spoiled. I realise that now.'

Maggie patted my hand.

'You're a good girl now, and my bet is that you were a good girl then too. Maybe the goodness was just buried more deeply before.'

Now it was my turn to be embarrassed.

'Anyway,' I said. 'I did exactly as you suggested, and I tried to help people, and doing that distracted me, and it helped me through some really hard times and ...'

Suddenly Maggie had her head in her hands.

'Oh no,' she wailed.

'What is it?' I said.

She looked up at me. 'I told you to help people.'

'Yes, and?'

'That's why you've been helping Ruby.'

Now I felt kind of guilty, like I'd been discovered doing something bad.

'Not exactly,' I said. 'Well ... maybe a bit. Maybe ...'

'Maybe what?'

Suddenly I felt like Maggie had vanished and I was looking at Madam Margarita again.

I felt like she could see through me – like she could tell what I was thinking even before I knew that I was thinking it.

Suddenly, lying didn't seem like such a good idea.

'OK,' I said, working it out in my head for the first time, as I spoke. 'In the beginning I helped Ruby because of what you said – because I thought that helping Ruby would help me. But after a while, that changed. I helped her because I wanted to help her. Helping her made me happy too.'

Maggie was smiling at me.

'That's very sweet of you, Eva,' she said. 'I appreciate that very much. You see, Ruby's never had many friends.'

Was she my friend?

'And I know she might not be your friend,' she continued, like she could read my mind. 'But you've been good to her, and that's the next best thing.'

I wasn't sure that I agreed with her. I couldn't imagine life without friends. I couldn't imagine how I'd survive without Victoria or Ella.

Maggie continued.

'Sometimes I think Ruby doesn't even want friends. She's always been like that, even before my accident and before our lives went a bit crazy.

I think it's just the way she is, and nothing is ever going to change that.'

Just then Ruby came back into the room.

'Lunch is ready,' she said. Then she stared at us. 'What's going on?' she asked. 'You both look very serious.'

I grinned and reached for the goldfish bowl.

'Maggie's thinking of taking up fortune-telling again. Fill the washing-up basin, Bubbles is coming in.'

The expression on Ruby's face went from shock to anger and back to shock.

'I'm kidding,' I said, and then the three of us laughed for a long time.

✩ ♥ ♡

Suddenly time seemed to start flying by.

Ella, Chloe and Amy came to the market and bought Maggie's bracelets and necklaces. They told their friends, and their friends told their friends. One weekend, the local newspaper ran a big article about Maggie (managing not to include details of her brief career as a fortune-teller) and soon Maggie couldn't keep up with the demand for her jewellery. After a while she had to get one of Mum's new friends to help her, and every afternoon, the two of them sat around the table in Maggie's house, making bracelets and having a laugh.

One day I came home from school to see Mum and Dad standing in the hallway giggling like teenagers.

'What's up?' I asked.

'Nothing,' they said, giggling even more.

'Whatever,' I said. '*Be* totally embarrassing. Don't let me stop you. I'm going upstairs to do my homework.'

They followed me upstairs and when I opened my bedroom door they were there to catch my bag as I dropped it to the floor.

'Omigod!' I gasped.

The walls of my room were no longer muddy brown. They were painted in wide stripes of bright pink and white.

'I got the paint cheaply,' said Dad proudly. 'It was left over after a big job.'

The ugly carpet was gone, and the floorboards underneath had been polished until they shone. Next to the bed was a beautiful bright pink and white rug.

'I made it myself,' said Mum. 'Out of scraps of fabric. My friend Deirdre showed me how.'

I hugged them both until they begged for mercy.

'We love you, Princess,' said Dad.

'I love you too,' I said. 'But, Dad ...'

'But what?'

'You can call me Eva.'

Chapter Twenty-Five

For my thirteenth birthday, I didn't have a pamper day in a big fancy hotel near my house. (For one thing, the big fancy hotel closed down months ago.)

Instead, some of my friends came over to my place and we ate pizza (topped with the first of Mum's homegrown tomatoes) and watched a DVD. Victoria was there of course, and Ella, and Amy and Chloe and a few other girls from my class. I invited Ruby, but she couldn't come. She was taking part in a long-distance swimming competition.

I didn't get my hair highlighted for my party. I

haven't been able to afford highlights for ages and ages, and my old highlights grew out a long time ago. I didn't have to go to my party looking like a swamp monster, though. Ruby's sister Jenny, who's a trainee hairdresser, came over in the morning and cut my hair for me, and tied it up so it looked really nice.

I didn't have a manicure either, but Victoria lent me some really nice nail varnish instead. We had fun painting our nails all kind of crazy colours.

Mum made me a double-chocolate birthday cake, and even though it was a little bit lop-sided, it was totally delicious. When I blew out the candles, Dad kept making stupid jokes that weren't even funny.

In the end I pretended to be cross.

'Make one more pathetic embarrassing joke and I'll start to wish that you were away on a business trip,' I said.

Dad hugged me and pretended to be hurt.

He kissed my cheek and I pretended that I thought that was gross.

We were both very glad that he was there.

☆ ❤ ♡

Victoria slept over that night. It was a bit of a squash in my tiny bedroom, but we didn't mind.

When we put the lights out, we were quiet for a long time.

'What are you thinking about?' I asked after a while.

'Nothing. What about you?'

'Nothing.'

I lay for another while, picturing our heads empty of thoughts – full instead of cotton wool or swirling grey smoke.

Then Victoria gave a big sigh.

'OK, I admit it. That was a lie. I was thinking about your party last year.'

I joined her in an even bigger sigh.

'Me too,' I said.

'An awful lot has happened to you since then.'

'Tell me about it,' I said.

'It hasn't been all bad, has it?' she asked.

'Hasn't it?' I asked, not really sure of the answer.

'Of course not,' said Victoria. 'Think of all the interesting people you met this year.'

'Like?'

If Victoria wanted to be the optimist in this friendship, maybe I should make her work hard for the honour.

She giggled.

'Like Madam Margarita for starters. How is she anyway?'

'Great. She seems really happy. She's making heaps of jewellery.'

'And you met Ruby this year.'

'That's true. And I forgot to tell you, she texted me earlier. She came second in her swimming competition. She says she might even join a swimming club if she keeps winning.'

Victoria laughed.

'She'd better be careful. If she goes on like this, soon she won't be weird any more.'

'And I got a postcard from Dawn yesterday. Remember the assistant in my class?'

Victoria giggled again.

'How could I forget? Did she ever find out how you helped her to escape?'

'I don't think so. I know she suspects something, but she can't figure out exactly what happened. Anyway, she's having a brilliant time in Peru, and then she's going to Bolivia.'

'That sounds so cool. And don't forget, you met Ella this year too. She's really nice. If you'd stayed in your old school you'd never have got to know her.'

I nodded, which was probably a bit stupid as Victoria couldn't see me in the dark.

'You know her dad's my teacher?'

'You only told me about a thousand times.'

I laughed.

'Whatever. Anyway, guess what he wrote in my last report?'

'What?'

'He said "Eva is the most helpful girl I have ever had the pleasure to teach."'

Then we both laughed until our faces hurt.

☆ ♥ ♡

That's the end of my story – for now.

If this was a fable, this is the bit where I should be describing what I've learned during the last year.

I should be saying that I now know that money isn't everything – that even though I'm poorer than I used to be, I'm happier that I've ever been before.

But unfortunately, life isn't a fable, or at least my life isn't anyway.

Last week Victoria told me that soon she's

going on a trip to Venice with the Pony Club. They're going to stay in a gorgeous hotel, have trips in gondolas, and eat yummy Italian ice-cream until it comes out their ears.

I smiled and hugged her.

I said that I hoped she had a totally fantastic time.

And then I went home and threw myself on my lumpy bed and cried until I ran out of tears.

One day recently I walked past my old house, Castleville. It was the first time I'd been there in ages. The electric gates were open, and I could see right inside.

I looked up at my old bedroom. The window was half-open and I could see my mauve curtains fluttering in the breeze. I could see a little girl sitting on the window seat, combing her hair.

She looked happy.

Was I happy for her?

No way!

I felt like running in through the gates, and up the stairs. I felt hauling her from the window seat and shaking her. I felt like telling her that the joke was over – that it was my house and it was time for her to leave.

How dare she steal my life and live my dreams?

But I really don't want to do time in a juvenile detention centre, so I turned my back on my beautiful old home. I walked up the road and after a minute I couldn't stand it any more. I clenched my fists and kicked a wall as hard as I possibly could.

It didn't make me feel any better, and a week later, I still had bruises on my toes.

So if this is a fable, it isn't a very good one – the moral is that kicking walls when you're wearing flip-flops really isn't a very good idea.

✯ ❤ ♡

So maybe my life isn't a fable, but could it be a fairy-tale?

If this was a fairy-tale, this is the bit where I should be saying how a miracle happened and I got my old life back.

If this was a fairy-tale, I should be once again living happily ever after in my old house, like the bad stuff had only been a terrible dream.

But life isn't a fairy-tale, or at least my life isn't anyway.

If this were a fairy-tale, the dad would be driving around in a golden carriage.

My dad drives around in a battered old van. He has converted heaps of attics. He says no one can afford to move house any more, so when they need more space they have to call on someone like him.

Dad doesn't dream of golden carriages or fancy cars any more, but if business continues like this, he says he might be able to buy a better van next year.

If this were a fairy-tale, the mum would sit

around on a throne, polishing her diamonds and rubies.

My mum sits around the kitchen a lot, chatting with the neighbours and swapping recipes and gardening tips. They're thinking of getting together to run an allotment.

Mum has more friends now than she had when she was living behind the high walls of Castleville.

Mum and her new friends don't wear gold-trimmed cloaks, but they laugh a lot.

So I think it's plain to see – my life is no fairy-tale any more.

But who wants to live in a fairy-tale anyway?

Those golden thrones look awfully uncomfortable.

Those handsome princes always look a bit skinny to me.

Those enchanted castles look cold and draughty.

And without electricity, how would I ever straighten my hair?

☆ ❤ ♡

It's been a very long year.

I've cried a lot and laughed a lot and lived a lot.

And what have I learned during these last twelve months?

1. I'm never going to be good at maths.

2. Turnips are cheap and strawberries aren't.

3. Even if you're not a princess, you can live happily ever after.

And that's exactly what I plan to do.

Best friends NEED to be together. Don't they?

Poor Megan! Not only is she stuck with totally uncool parents, and a little sister who is too cute for words, but now her best friend, Alice, has moved away. Now Megan has to go to school and face the dreaded Melissa all on her own.
The two friends hatch a risky plot to get back together. But can their secret plan work?

It's mid-term break and Megan's off to visit Alice.

Megan is hoping for a nice trouble-free few days with her best friend. No such luck! She soon discovers that Alice is once again plotting and scheming.
It seems that Alice's mum Veronica has a new boy-friend. The plan is to discover who he is, and to get rid of him!

Alice and Megan are together again!

They are both looking forward to their Confirmation, especially as their two families are going out to dinner together to celebrate.
But not even a meal can be simple when Alice is around as she decides to hatch a plan to get her parents back together ...

Best friends forever?

Megan can't wait to go away
to Summer Camp with Alice!
It will be fantastic – no organic porridge, no school, nothing but fun! But when Alice makes friends with Hazel, Megan begins to feel left out. Hazel's pretty, sophisticated and popular, and Alice seems to think she's amazing.
Is Megan going to lose her very best friend?

Sunshine & yummy French food – sounds like the perfect holiday!

Megan's really looking forward to the summer holidays – her whole family is going to France, and best of all Alice is coming too! But when Alice tries to make friends with a local French boy things begin to get very interesting ...

How much should you give up for your best friend?

Alice has a good chance of winning the school essay competition – and the prize is four months in France!

Megan loves writing essays, but she'd hate to go away for four months alone! She doesn't want Alice to go either – why would anyone want to go abroad without her best friend? But Alice seems determined to win ...

WHY NOT VISIT THE GREAT NEW 'ALICE & MEGAN' WEBSITE AT WWW.OBRIEN.IE/ALICEANDMEGAN
www.obrien.ie

Latest Judi news, new books, events, free stuff!
Exclusive sneak peeks
'Ask Judi'
Sign up to receive the special 'Alice & Megan' newsletter
Great competitions and freebies
Reader Review – become an online reviewer ... and much more!

www.judicurtin.com
News
'Diary of an Author'
Updates on all Judi's books!